"Caitlan, something is happening here, between us," John said in a voice that shook with emotion.

"But I don't want it to." He felt the warmth of her body pressed against his and began to tremble. Her touch was turning him into whipped cream. He ached for her. And he couldn't hold back any longer.

Caitlan moaned as he lowered his lips to kiss her. Her heart pounded wildly as the roar of passion swept through them.

"I want you, Caitlan Downey. I've never wanted a woman so much in my life. I'm going crazy being so close without touching you. I want to make love to you, to hear all those love sounds you whisper when you're nursing the baby."

"I know," she said, "but this isn't real. It's an illusion. You know, motherhood, the caveman and his mate. I don't think you want me for me, John. You want me because you're here and I'm here. Let's not hurt each other."

He pulled her to him with a fierce and loving look. "You're wrong, Caitlan. I could never hurt you. Never." And with his lips he began teaching her to love him. . . .

WHAT ARE *LOVESWEPT* ROMANCES?

They are stories of true romance and touching emotion. We believe those two very important ingredients are constants in our highly sensual and very believable stories in the *LOVESWEPT* line. Our goal is to give you, the reader, stories of consistently high quality that may sometimes make you laugh, sometimes make you cry, but are always fresh and creative and contain many delightful surprises within their pages.

Most romance fans read an enormous number of books. Those they truly love, they keep. Others may be traded with friends and soon forgotten. We hope that each *LOVESWEPT* romance will be a treasure—a "keeper." We will always try to publish

*LOVE STORIES YOU'LL NEVER FORGET
BY AUTHORS YOU'LL ALWAYS REMEMBER*

The Editors

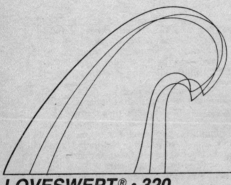

LOVESWEPT® • 320

Sandra Chastain
The Silver Bullet
Affair

 BANTAM BOOKS
TORONTO • NEW YORK • LONDON • SYDNEY • AUCKLAND

THE SILVER BULLET AFFAIR
A Bantam Book / April 1989

If you would be interested in receiving protective vinyl
covers for your Loveswept books, please write to this address
for information:

Loveswept
Bantam Books
P.O. Box 985
Hicksville, NY 11802

ISBN 0-553-21967-7

Published simultaneously in the United States and Canada

PRINTED IN THE UNITED STATES OF AMERICA

O   0 9 8 7 6 5 4 3 2 1

For Marion, Shannon, Donna, and Nancy who were there when I stepped on the carousel and stayed with me for the ride

One

Take care of Caitlan and the baby. It's mine.
Jeff

John Garmon stood at the door with Jeffrey's two-line note in his hand, turning it over and over. Though he'd seen little of it in the last five years, the handwriting was unmistakably that of his brother.

Caitlan Downey, the pregnant girl who had been so grief stricken at the funeral of her sister, Ann, and brother-in-law, Jeffrey, the girl who impulsively had hugged him and rested her head on his chest in an expression of shared grief, had been left in his care through Jeffrey's will.

Oh, yes, he knew who Caitlan Downey was. She was the tiny, fragile girl with the doe eyes who had made an impact on his body with her touch and on his mind with her pain. Afterward she'd disappeared.

Two things struck John Garmon when Caitlan opened the door of the Florida beach cottage. She wasn't pregnant any longer, and she could never be called a girl. The barefoot woman with wet hair and no makeup standing in the doorway was beautiful. The stubborn jut of her chin and proud tilt of her head marked her dismay as she looked up at him.

"Oh, Mr. Garmon, I'm sorry. I was in the shower." She tried to make her voice sound casual but friendly. "What are you doing here?"

He set off a six-alarm fire bell in Caitlan Downey's head, and she swallowed hard to push back the panic that swept over her. Wearing dark glasses and a butter-colored silk jacket, John Garmon looked like a model for the cover of some famous travel magazine. Just under six feet tall, he had the lean, powerful build of a swimmer. His burnished gold hair was layered short in front, longer in back, where it touched the collar of his pale blue shirt. A thick gold bracelet circled the tanned wrist of the hand in which he held an envelope.

When he spoke, his voice had a warm, moonlight-and-magnolias quality to it that made her toes tingle and sent chills up her spine.

"I think you know the reason for my visit, don't you, Ms. Downey? May I come in?"

Caitlan shrugged her shoulders and motioned him inside. She was sunk, she thought. A posse couldn't have corralled her any more completely than John Garmon had done by simply standing in her doorway. What a wonderful analogy. She was thinking like Billy the Kid when she was dealing with George Hamilton without a suntan.

Adjusting the tie at the waist of the white terry cloth robe she'd hastily pulled on when she heard the doorbell ring, she trailed the man as he walked slowly into her living room, thinking furiously as she walked. Six months had passed, and she still wasn't ready to face the Garmon family—certainly not John Garmon. They were the reason why she'd fled Georgia.

John Garmon was silk shirts and Italian shoes. She was cotton sundresses and flip-flops. They had nothing in common except her secret, and she was bound to keep that, no matter what. Her thoughts whirled through her head like a crazy kaleidoscope of color as she watched the smooth, self-assured man walk around her little beach house.

"Will you excuse me for a moment while I get a towel for my hair?"

Caitlan didn't wait for his answer. She ran into the bedroom and closed the door, leaning heavily against it. Her knees were weak and her breath was irregular. Oh, Lordy, she thought, the man was everything she remembered him to be and more, and she hadn't even looked into his eyes yet. The only difference was that his effect on her was even more astounding than it had been at the funeral. Her pulse had raced for days after their first encounter.

"He isn't the enemy, for heaven's sake," Caitlan whispered to herself, fighting the panic his presence evoked. He was just a man, Jeffrey's brother. Ann had liked him. She'd even hoped that the estrangement between their two families would end—then the accident had changed everything. Caitlan threaded her fingers through her hair and considered her next move. At least little Caity was with the sitter.

Why should she panic over the fact that John Garmon had come after her. She'd known the possibility existed that he or someone in the family would find her, but she'd hoped the someone would be a stranger, some strictly-business attorney who'd say he represented the Garmon family interests and had come to straighten out an unacceptably tangled situation. She paced back and forth considering her defense.

Business, strictly business, that's how she'd handle this meeting. It wouldn't take long.

"Hello, Ms. Downey? Are you all right?" John called from the other room.

All right? No, she most definitely was not all right. But there was precious little she could do about it except face the inevitable. One thing Caitlan Downey had never been was a coward.

"Caitlan, are you still in there?"

His voice was growing insistent. She knew how thorough he was, how organized, how insistent. Jeffrey had told her. Any minute now he'd probably break down her door and . . .

Caitlan grabbed a towel and returned to the living room, rubbing her hair vigorously. At least she could cover her face and keep a guarded watch on him as they talked. She didn't have a lot of time to talk. She had to get back to work. "Certainly I'm still here. Where else would I be?"

John Garmon frowned at her as though he wanted to say something stern. The minute he'd seen her, he knew he'd made a mistake. He should have sent Lint, his attorney. John glanced casually around the room, then walked over to the bedroom door and peered inside. Business, it was simply a business matter, he told himself. Focusing on the problem was how he'd handle the woman wearing only a white robe standing primly before him.

Oh, hell, he was in big trouble and he knew it. He hadn't expected her to look like some fragile siren from the sea. His body's reaction indicated that what he wanted to do was wrap her in his arms and take care of her.

"Where else would you be? That's a laugh. You're like quicksilver, Ms. Downey. You seem to be very good at disappearing. It's taken me six months to find you. Are we alone?"

"Why? Aren't your intentions honorable?"

John jerked around to look at her. Her voice was deep with a Garbolike hoarseness. He'd thought about that voice. He'd wondered if its depth came from the emotional loss she'd experienced or whether it was normal. For weeks the memory of the sound of her voice had drifted around him like some kind of elusive perfume, like a half-remembered show tune that refused to leave his head.

"Frankly, my dear"—he forced himself to respond lightly, as he leaned back against the door frame and folded his arms across his chest—"I left my Jack-the-Ripper bag back in Savannah."

Could the man have a sense of humor? Or was he mocking her? "Please sit down, Mr. Garmon." Caitlan suddenly dropped to the floor and sat with her legs crossed. She leaned forward to rub briskly at her thick, black hair, which hung down like a velvet waterfall. "I don't believe in formality or beating around the bush, so state your intentions. I don't have much time."

"Fine!" He dropped to the floor beside her, feeling a distinct rise in the temperature on the way down. "Neither do I." He'd better keep his mind on the problem he'd come to solve, before his thoughts got out of hand, he told himself.

"Well?" she prompted.

"Let's talk about you and my brother," he said sharply, trying not to see the soft swell of bare breast peeking from the vee of her robe as she rubbed her hair. "Did you love him?"

He didn't know why he'd asked the question. He hadn't intended to take such a direct approach, but the woman had confused him. He admitted that he wanted—no, needed—to know the answer to this question.

She flung her hair back across her shoulders. Her smile this time was bittersweet and even more brief. "Oh, yes. Everybody loved Jeffrey. He . . . he was . . . special," she stammered.

He should have looked stern and out of place, sitting on the sand-colored carpet in her living room in a jacket and tie, but he didn't. He simply looked as if he'd struck a different pose for another magazine cover. He leaned closer as though he was waiting for her to say more.

"Why did you come here?"

"Because I have friends here," she answered, "and I think you ought to know that they've probably already passed on the information via their beach hot line to my gang that I have a strange man in my cottage."

She seemed uneasy, but she definitely wasn't afraid. As absurd as it sounded, he thought she might even be teasing him. The soft smile she'd given him when he asked about Jeffrey made her look elfin, almost innocent. And he already knew that she was anything but innocent. In fact, he was becoming more certain that she was somehow putting him on with her warning.

He laughed.

Caitlan had the feeling that if he'd had a mustache he'd have twirled it.

John cleared his throat. "Your gang? I see. What are you, an outlaw?"

"I've been called that," she admitted. "I steal from the rich and give to the poor."

"I believe you, and I'm the Lone Ranger, hot on your trail."

He did look a little as if he were wearing a mask. The dark glasses concealed his eyes, and she was glad. He'd been wearing them at the cemetery too. It wasn't until afterward at the Garmon home that he'd removed them. His blue eyes were as vivid as she'd remembered them. The first time he'd looked at her, she'd felt an unmistakable shift in the mantle of the earth, and it had set off tremors every time their gazes had met. She suddenly knew that even if she hadn't already planned to, she'd better get out of Dodge—quick!

"Well, Kemo Sabe," she said, "I'm not in need of rescue, and you're not wearing a white hat. So, state your business and vamoose. I've got to get ready for work."

"Work?" He jerked his glasses off. The sudden light spilling in through the sliding glass doors caused his pupils to open wide, changing his expression to one of stern disbelief.

"Yes, work. That effort extended in return for monetary gain. You know—money, the stuff we need to live. I'm a nurse, remember, and I'm due back at the hospital soon. Why are you really here?"

"I came to check on you, Ms. Downey."

"Why?" She knew her voice was breathless. There

was a whirlwind churning inside her chest, swirling a riptide of emotion around and around. Having to look up at him was putting her at a distinct disadvantage. He was almost a foot taller than she, and from the floor he looked like a god, a vengeful god. She scrambled to her knees with the intention of rising.

John Garmon moved forward also, and for a moment their knees touched. He took her hand and came lithely to his feet, lifting her as he stood.

Standing was a mistake. She was nose to chest with the man who was turning her insides to warm honey. In order to talk to him she had to lift her head, and that placed her in the perfect position to be kissed. She heard him take a deep breath and let it out. She could feel his breath on her forehead, and she fought the urge to lay her cheek on his shoulder and feel his arms around her as she'd done at the funeral.

She took a step back and began to run her fingers through her hair, separating the strands and arranging them down her back like a black lacey fan. "Why did you come all this way to check on me, Mr. Garmon?" she asked again.

"You were living with my brother and your sister. You're Jeffrey's sister-in-law." He looked down at her for a very long moment. "That's only partly true. I came because I couldn't get you out of my mind after the funeral. I was . . . worried about you."

She dropped the towel and concentrated on the soft white tasseled loafers he was wearing while she stood like an ice statue. "Why?"

"Because you were pregnant, dammit. I know about the baby."

For a moment everything tilted crazily and then fell back into place. She'd known from the beginning that it would be John Garmon who would come after her. And now he was there in her little beach house, larger than life and much too close. She knew the reaction she was having was because of the man himself, not his question, but the question had to be answered sooner or later.

"How'd you find me?"

"It wasn't easy. Everybody in Pretty Springs, Georgia seemed to know you, but nobody would tell me where you'd gone. If it hadn't been for some chubby do-gooder named Harold who worked at the nursing home with you, I'd never have found you."

"Harold told you. It figures. Harold always was a sucker for families because he never had one. Is Harold all right?"

"He seemed fine as far as I could tell, but he's worried about you. Everyone there is worried about you. Even the sheriff threatened me with jail if I harmed you. And some blond amazon named Kaylyn said to tell you that the Lizard is fine and that she'd picket the chocolate factory if you wanted her to." John shook his head. The woman before him was remarkable. She couldn't weigh more than a hundred pounds. Her dark hair was drying into a fine halo around her small face. Her luminous dark eyes had been veiled, wary until they came suddenly alive with the mention of an old man named Harold and a town called Pretty Springs. Now he could see little flecks of silver in her eyes that glistened like danger signals in the night. "What did you do in that town, walk on water?"

"Me? No, I just cared about the people, I guess."

"I thought that was my brother's self-appointed mission in life." He realized his voice sounded angry and accusing, as it had so many times when he'd talked to his brother. Give ole' John a business deal and he'd handle it, he thought self-deprecatingly. Give him a situation involving somebody he cared about and he'd blow it every time.

"Jeff, Ann," Caitlan said softly, "I . . . we all loved them, and they loved us." Caitlan glanced at her watch. "I'm sorry, Mr. Garmon, but I do have to get dressed for work."

"Fine," he agreed. "Leave the door open a crack and we can talk while you dress."

"I don't think we have anything to talk about." She started toward the bedroom.

"But we do, Ms. Downey. For starters, what have you done with Jeffrey's baby?"

The air whooshed out of her lungs and she swayed, catching the door frame for support. He didn't just know about the baby. He knew that it was Jeffrey's baby. "Who told you?"

"Jeffrey told me."

"I don't believe you."

"Would you believe his own handwriting? I don't know what happened between you and my brother, Ms. Downey, but it seems our family has both a legal and a moral obligation to look after you. Jeffrey left you provided for. None of that is as important as this note, however. Jeffrey seems to have added a little personal codicil to his will.

Caitlan turned slowly around and stared wide-eyed at him. Was he trying to trick her for some reason she didn't understand? She'd been sworn to secrecy. She'd expected Jeffrey to comply with the decision he himself had made. Why would he reveal half the truth? She didn't know, and she wasn't going to admit to anything—yet.

"The baby is mine, Mr. Garmon. You don't need to concern yourself with us."

"Perhaps you can enlighten me, Ms. Downey." His voice turned to steel. Letting anger come to the fore was the only way he could keep himself from taking her into his arms. "According to this note, my brother very clearly asked me to watch out for you and the child. I don't understand his will and I don't understand the note, but let's not kid each other, Ms. Downey, ma'am. I definitely have to be concerned with you. Maybe you'd like to explain."

John Garmon held out the note. Caitlan's fingers brushed his as she took it, and she jerked her hand away as though the heat of his touch had seared her. She glanced at him quickly to see if he'd noticed her reaction and groaned inwardly as she realized he had.

There was no explanation, no direction to the note, only the request that John Garmon look after her. The lazy scrawl was definitely Jeffrey's handwriting. It wasn't the request that shocked her, but the last three words, "the baby's mine," that caused the blood to rush from her head to her feet. For the first time in her life she felt faint, and without realizing what she was doing, she reached out to John Garmon.

"We agreed not to tell."

John responded automatically, placing both hands on Caitlan's shoulders, supporting her, studying her as if he couldn't understand her words. "Why?"

"We didn't want anyone to know."

"You were having my brother's baby and you didn't want anyone to know? What did your sister think?"

Caitlan looked up at the man holding her. What was she to do? Jeffrey already had told him part of the truth. If Jeff wanted him to know, what right did she have to keep the secret now?"

"My having the baby was Ann's idea. She couldn't give Jeffrey a child. I was carrying it as a gift, my gift to them. Now please leave, Mr. Garmon. I do have to get to work." She had to get away from him, to think out what she should do now that the secret had been exposed.

"A surrogate mother? I'm not leaving until I get a more detailed explanation."

"Fine! Stay as long as you like. There's food in the fridge and the door is always open. But don't be surprised if part of my 'gang' stops by to check you out while I'm gone."

Caitlan whirled around and mechanically walked into the bedroom. She switched on her hair dryer. At least if John Garmon talked, she wouldn't be able to hear him. Thank heavens Caity wasn't there, she thought. She didn't want him to see her baby if she could prevent it. Caity was such a beautiful child that once John Garmon saw her he'd never leave.

At last her hair was dry. She caught it in her hand and twisted it skillfully into a figure eight at the base of her neck and pinned it securely. Donning white hose, sturdy shoes, and a crisp white uniform, she was satisfied that she looked confident and in charge. Giving a last-minute sweep of peach-colored blush to her cheeks and a coat of soft color to her lips, she was ready. The final ritual was pinning her tiny coronet-shaped nurse's cap to the top of her head.

Most nurses had quickly abandoned the cap. Most

hospitals no longer required it to be worn. But to Caitlan the tiny little white starched crown was the badge of her success and her authority. She was proud to wear it, and she never reported for duty without her cap. Fully dressed in her uniform, she stepped back into the living room.

John was standing on the deck, gazing off into the distance. As she walked through the open sliding glass doors, he turned toward her.

"You look very nice, and efficient."

"Thanks, I am. I take my nursing duties very seriously."

"Isn't it a bit soon for you to be going back to work? I mean, how old is the child, two or three months?"

"Three and a half," she corrected automatically, "and I . . ." She started to say that she had to, that she needed the money for Caity. But she finished her sentence with, "I only work part-time, three days a week."

"Then you haven't given the child to someone else?"

"Given Caity away?" Caitlan was speechless for a moment. "What kind of mother do you think I am? Of course I haven't given her away. I love my baby."

"A little girl. Named for you, I presume?"

"She's Caitlan Ann. I'm glad you approve."

"Just how long will you be gone," John asked, glancing at his watch as if he had a schedule to meet and she was deliberately throwing him off.

"I usually work the midnight shift."

"But it's two o'clock in the afternoon."

"I know, I'm taking part of the shift of my friend Daisy so she can attend her son's college graduation. I came home to shower and change clothes, and now I have to get back to the highway to hitch a ride to the hospital."

"To do what?" he asked incredulously.

"Well, I used to ride my bicycle, but now I usually ride with Lieutenant Kelly who patrols the beach. This isn't his shift, so I'll just walk up to the highway. Sooner or later somebody I know will come along and pick me up. I have lots of friends."

John groaned in disbelief. The mother of his brother's child hitchhiked to work? Why not? he asked himself, she had to be . . . different. Different was the only word he could come up with as he took in her cool, efficient appearance. Efficient, yes, he thought, but he was having trouble erasing the picture of her shapely legs crossed beneath her earlier as she sat on the floor drying her hair. The thick terry cloth material hadn't hidden the full breasts that had spilled out from the center of the robe as she'd raised and lowered her arms, and the crisp uniform did little to conceal them.

Caitlan Downey was a nursing mother—nursing mother alone, on her own, if his report was right—and nothing about the cottage suggested the presence of a man. He'd looked around carefully while she was dressing. Although he knew there was nothing unusual about a single woman having a child, he felt very strongly that a child needed a father—he'd grown up without one. But the little girl wasn't just any child, she was Jeffrey's baby. Caitlan had wanted to give Jeffrey and Ann a special gift, but they'd been killed in a boating accident before the child was born. Afterward Caitlan had taken her gift and disappeared.

"No hitchhiking today, Caitlan. I'll drive you."

"Oh, no, that won't be necessary. I'd planned to stop back by the nursery in time to feed Caity and spend some time with her before reporting in." She looked at her watch and gasped. "All right," she agreed, rather than waste more time arguing, "Let's go."

The car had Garmon written all over it. It was an expensive black sports car with leather seats and tinted windows that hid its occupants from the world. Caitlan got in and closed her door quickly, before John could assist her.

"Which way?"

"Go left on the beach highway and head back toward the strip. I'll tell you when to turn. May I open the window?"

"Certainly. Though most women want the windows closed so the wind won't spoil their hair."

"Not me. I like the feel of the ocean breeze. It's cool and fresh. If it spoils my hair, I'll just twist it up again."

The carnival rides on the pier crowded the skyline, and the midsummer traffic began to slow. She'd forgotten about the traffic caused by the tourists early in the day. Riding with Lieutenant Kelly was easy. They traveled late at night and in his police car they had no trouble getting through without interference. Caitlan glanced at her watch. She shifted her arms. Her breasts were full and growing uncomfortable. It was past time to nurse her child.

"Turn at the next light," she said, impatient now with her close proximity to John Garmon. "The hospital is on the right."

As John Garmon turned the sports car into the drive, Caitlan caught a glimpse of Danni's little orange Honda sitting in traffic in the opposite lane.

"Quick! Blow your horn!" she said as she leaned across a startled John and blasted the horn repeatedly. "Damn! She won't recognize me in this car." Caitlan opened the door and waved as Danni's car shot past them.

"What in hell are you doing?" John Garmon yelled as he watched the orange car come to a stop in the traffic and saw Caitlan Downey thread her way across two lanes to the other side. She opened the car door, leaned inside to converse for a moment, then backed away with her arms full and stood aside as the orange car pulled away amid the honking of car horns and drivers' curses. By the time John maneuvered his car across to the inside lane, Caitlan was standing on the side of the road holding a shoulder bag and a baby.

He pulled up beside her. "Get in!"

"That's all right," she assured him, and turned to walk in the opposite direction. "I can walk from here."

John set the emergency brake, left the car with the engine running, and strode angrily after her. "I said, get in. I'll take you where you have to go!"

This time Caitlan obeyed his directive. His tone of voice told her that if she didn't, he'd pick her up, baby and all, and carry her.

"Now," he said, then took a deep breath, eased the car into traffic, and drove silently for a long moment. "Suppose you tell me what in hell you were doing back there."

"Well, normally, if I don't make it to the nursery before my friend Danni leaves, she takes Caity home with her. Now I'll just leave the baby in the nursery until morning."

"Why didn't you notify this woman Danni?"

"Oh, I tried. But she was at breakfast when I left the hospital, and my phone is . . . Well, I planned to make it back to the nursery to feed Caity before I reported in."

The baby began to whimper and nuzzle insistently against Caitlan's white uniform. Even to a novice it was obvious that the child was demanding to be fed. Caitlan uncovered the baby's small face and made loving little sounds as she kissed her. But the child had no intention of being comforted. She was hungry, and soon her whimper turned into a furious demand.

"Please, turn around and take me back to the nursery so I can feed her. It's the small yellow building past the main facility." Caitlan closed the windows and prayed that he'd hurry.

But Caity did not intend to wait, and John Garmon seemed disinclined to rush. "I'm sorry, Mr. Garmon, but I'm afraid that she's not going to wait. I'll feed her now, if you don't mind. I mean, with these dark windows, nobody will be able to see what I'm doing." She began to unbutton her uniform.

John kept his eyes forward and nodded, unwilling to trust himself to answer. From the moment he'd caught a glimpse of the child, he'd felt his breath leave his body. She was only a baby, and although he'd always thought all babies looked alike, this child was exquisite. Rebellious lungs demanded attention, and he smiled at the way such a tiny person could force an adult to comply with her wishes. Then he heard the satisfied sounds of her nursing.

He wouldn't intrude on the private moment between mother and child. He wouldn't look, he told himself even as he was turning his head. He gasped. The soft amber sunlight filtered through the opaque window, falling over the woman and child like the special effects in a movie. The baby laid one tiny clenched fist against her mother's full breast while she suckled contentedly. With her eyes closed, Caitlan rested her chin against her child's head.

John Garmon stopped the car and stared. He'd never seen a lovelier sight. From deep inside he felt a tightening that clasped his chest and moved toward his lower body in a wave of longing. He was attracted to this woman in a way he'd never experienced before. He wanted to put his arms around her and hold both her and the child while the baby nursed. He gripped the wheel hard, took a deep breath, and averted his gaze before he gave in to the impulse to reach out and feel the tiny fist clasp his finger.

The sound of motion and the child's cry of displeasure reclaimed his attention before he realized what he was doing. Caitlan looked at him sternly and pulled her uniform to cover herself as she lifted the child to her shoulder and patted her back.

"She has to be burped," Caitlan explained, her words clipped and her cheeks aflame.

"I guess I don't know much about babies," John admitted, not bothering to turn his head away as she pulled the uniform open and shielded herself as best she could, shifting the child to her other breast.

"If you're quite finished staring, you can drive around to the side of the building and let me out. I'll take Caity back to the nursery and report for duty."

She was brash, stubborn, and modest. He liked those qualities. In fact, he was finding he liked a lot about the woman he'd been commissioned to care for, the woman who had borne his brother's child.

"Uh, yes. Fine." John backed out of the parking space he'd found by the road and followed Caitlan's directions. "What time will you be finished here? I'll pick you up."

"I finish Daisy's shift at seven. I'll feed Caity and catch a few hours of sleep in the nurses' quarters. Kelly will bring me home in the morning."

"Kelly, as in Lieutenant Kelly?"

"Yes."

John stopped at the door Caitlan indicated and stared at her in stoney silence. Caitlan gently pulled the child away and slid her bra back over the breast, fastening the center clasp before buttoning the uniform once more.

"Thank you for the ride," she finally said, and gathered up the baby's bag and her purse. "And you're welcome to use the loft bedroom in my house tonight, if you like."

"I will. And I'll be here in the morning, and we'll talk about all this then."

The tension in the car was palpable, and Caitlan didn't know where it had come from. She'd never felt uncomfortable nursing her child before. Feeding the baby was a natural process, and her friends had watched her without making her feel all quivery and weightless inside. But being there with John Garmon was a new and disturbing situation. She could see he felt it too, in the way he gripped the wheel and forced himself to take long, even breaths.

Searching her mind, she looked for a way to dissolve the tension. She was behaving like a moon-faced thirteen-year-old. After all, he was Jeffrey's brother. Jeffrey always had spoken of John with love, and in the end, Jeffrey had revealed their secret to him. She'd give him the benefit of the doubt—for now. They shouldn't be enemies. They should be friends. If he was Jeffrey's brother, he had to be a nice person. John Garmon was certainly the best-looking man she'd seen in a long, long time, and he couldn't help it if he came across as stiff and demanding. He just needed love, she decided.

"All right, John," she said softly. "And, John"—impulsively she reached across the seat, caught his chin with her fingertips, and pulled him closer, kissing his cheek lightly—"thank you."

On the fourth floor of the hospital, Quinta Kelly, Lieutenant Kelly's wife, looked up from behind her supervisor's desk as Caitlan stepped off the elevator.

"Goodness, Caitlan, you look as if you just flew in on a rocket and your feet haven't touched the ground yet. What happened, did you finally hear from that man you've been waiting for?"

"Man I've been waiting for?" Caitlan swallowed back a quick denial, then smiled as she considered how accurate Quinta's observation was. "Maybe," she admitted, "maybe I have."

The fact that she sang to her patients that night wasn't unusual. What was different was that she sang Broadway show tunes instead of lullabies or songs about herding cattle. Caitlan Downey wasn't a theater person and she didn't listen to romantic music. She was more into cartoons and old cowboy movies.

When she offered to arrange a blind date between

old Mrs. Barton in 401 and Luke West in 412, she caught Quinta Kelly's amused giggle in the hallway behind her. It wasn't until she took a patient's temperature for the second time in five minutes that she admitted her mind was in the loft of her beach cottage—and her imagination was playing games.

By early morning her feet hurt, her breasts were tight with milk, and she was very tired. All she wanted to do was pick up her baby and go home, but John Garmon was waiting there, and she wasn't sure how she felt about that. All she knew was that when one of the nurses came in early and offered to return the two hours that Caitlan had worked for her last week, she grabbed the chance to leave. When Lieutenant Kelly wandered in and offered her a ride, Caitlan took it gratefully. Bone-weary, she picked up Caity from the nursery, then dozed in the backseat of the squad car as the child nursed all the way home. She was glad she didn't have to work again until the following week.

The smell of coffee greeted her as she stepped through the door. Coming home felt different to her, and the man who welcomed her was the reason. The feeling was good, she decided, very good.

Two

The first of Caitlan's "gang," Tony, the postman, began his casual interrogation shortly after John Garmon returned to the cabin. Tony delivered two overdue bills and a "mess" of spring onions and fresh squash to Caitlan from Mrs. Winslow who lived down the beach.

"Caitlan always looks in on Mr. Winslow since he broke his hip last month. They can't pay her, but they send her something every day or two. Are you sick, son, or are you out of a job?"

John Garmon stood in the kitchen watching the carrot-haired, uniformed man place the vegetables in Caitlan's refrigerator.

"Do I look sick or unemployed?" He knew his voice was unnecessarily stern, but he was unaccustomed to people entering someone's home without knocking. Apparently it was the accepted routine here.

"I'm Tony, by the way. And I didn't think you looked like one of the others." He nodded in satisfaction. "Tell Caitlan that Marsha Fielding over at the post office is paying her telephone bill. She's worried about Caitlan being out here without a working phone. Says Caitlan can pay her back when she's able."

"Others? What others?" John Garmon followed Tony back through the living room, out of the cottage, and up the walk to the road, where his Jeep was parked, the motor running.

"Oh, you know Caitlan. Anybody in need of food, a place to stay, or anything else she has is always welcome."

"Of course," John agreed dryly, "and speaking of welcome, aren't you delivering the mail awfully late in the day?"

"I made her my last stop so that I could deliver these vegetables. Usually I drop by in the morning too. That way I can run errands for her, if she needs anything. Hope you find whatever it is you're looking for, Mr. . . . What did you say your name was?"

"Garmon," John answered him sharply. He saw the startled look on Tony's face but attributed it to a reaction to his own undisguised anger. "And, yes, it appears that I've found what I'm looking for. Though I don't know what I'm going to do with her now that I've found her."

"Don't guess you want my advice, Garmon, but I'm going to give it to you anyway. Caitlan is special. We wouldn't take kindly to anybody bossing her around."

"Is that a threat?"

"Not yet." Tony released the brake on the Jeep and gave the engine enough gas to drown out the rest of his statement.

John watched him pull onto the highway, give a

wave that could be defined as something between a salute and an accusation, and drive away.

Damn! He'd discovered the same kind of protective circle of friends back in Pretty Springs when he'd tried to check on Caitlan Downey. She was regarded as being one step away from sainthood. John paced back and forth around the small beach house. It was well furnished, not at all what he'd expect a woman forced to return to work part-time to support her child could afford.

The mystery was cleared up by the next caller, Jeb McGraw, a seven-foot mountain of a man who owned the local bookstore. He came by to leave a message for Caitlan. He'd heard from Nita over at the rental office that the owners, the Boswells, were considering selling the cottage. Jeb thought he might have a lead an another family Caitlan could house-sit for. He looked John over thoroughly and before leaving commented that John was a day late, but from the looks of the wheels outside, he guessed he wasn't too many dollars short.

John decided that tomorrow he'd drive into town and have a little chat with Nita. He hadn't worked out all the details of what he was going to do about Caitlan, but until he'd made proper arrangements for Jeffrey's child, he didn't want anything disrupted. He already had had a sample of Caitlan Downey's stubbornness, but so far she had no idea of his own determination.

By early evening he'd made a quick stop on the strip for coffee and milk, had heard from Lieutenant Kelly, and had met a surly man who refused to leave his name saying only that he lived down the beach. Then a five-foot-tall character about thirteen years of age who called himself Dip and said he was on the lam had dropped by.

Between interruptions John examined the cottage carefully. If he hadn't seen the baby in Caitlan's arms he might have doubted her existence. Other than a package of disposable diapers in the bathroom, there wasn't a hint of the presence of a baby— not so much as a baby bed in the whole place. Buying a crib would be his second project. First, though, he'd figure out how to post off-limits signs to the population of the lower half of the southern states.

The bed in the loft was unmade, and he couldn't find the sheets. Caitlan probably had loaned them to some beach bum who needed sails for his boat. He tried sleeping in her bed but it felt too intimate. John Garmon finally spent a sleepless night on a couch that was six inches too short and rolled in on him in the middle. At dawn's first light he was up, making coffee and squeezing fresh oranges for juice.

The doorbell rang as he was taking his morning shower. Finally someone who rang the doorbell! he thought. He'd just stepped out of the stall and into the bathroom when he heard a woman's voice. "Hello? Anyone here?"

"Damn! His clothes were in the bedroom and if he could judge by the sound of the voice, so was the woman. Any minute she'd be in the bathroom with him. Caitlan's terry cloth robe hanging on the back of the door was his only choice. He thrust his arms into the garment and pulled it as tight as he could to cover his large frame.

"Caity Dee, are you already at home?"

The female voice stopped for a second at the bathroom door, then continued breathlessly. "Why didn't you tell me about your man? I thought that he . . . oops! Who are you?"

"I suppose you could say that I'm the man. Who are you?"

"I'm the meddling friend. What's your name?"

"Garmon. Yours?" John groaned. At the rate Caitlan's "gang" was arriving, he'd need Harold from the nursing home to keep score. The cottage was busier than Atlanta International Airport.

"I'm Danni Manderson. You ought to be ashamed of yourself, you devil, abandoning Caitlan in her hour of need. And you with all that money. I hope you've come to make an honest woman of her and give that child a name."

The woman was tall, blond, and very tan. She wore a lime-green fifties-style dress and some kind of rope sandals that wound around her legs to tie just below her knees. Dark glasses and dangling shell earrings peeked out from beneath an oversized straw hat that concealed her face and hair.

"Of course"—she began to walk slowly around him, studying him as though he were an original designer gown—"having your baby told us how she felt about you, but now I can see for myself why she was so infatuated with you that she's refused to date every man along the strip. Yes, you're quite a man, and that's an interesting robe you're almost wearing."

"The baby isn't mine—yet."

"Lighten up, Garmon. First you run out on her, now you've come to claim Caity? I ought to warn you that you'd better not hurt her again . . ."

"Why not warn me?" he muttered under his breath. "Everybody else has."

". . . or we'll string you up by your aristocratic knees and pull out your toenails one at a time. On second thought, you'd look great with an apple in your mouth. Maybe a barbecue would be better."

The woman was bonkers. The population of the whole Gulf Coast was heading toward complete insanity, he thought. John tugged unsuccessfully on the hem of Caitlan's robe while he tried to regain control of the situation.

It wasn't to be.

He heard someone cross the outer deck, and then the front door opened and slammed behind the intruder.

"Do come in," John called out, "no point in knocking, nobody else does." He turned in resignation to face his newest interrogator.

"John!" Caitlan stood in the doorway, wide-eyed with surprise, holding the child. She shot him a look that could have singed his eyebrows. "What's going on?"

"Caitlan, he's wonderful," Danni said, giving her friend a hug. "A little testy, but he's tough. I'm so happy for you. Let me get out of here so that you can be alone with this gorgeous, gorgeous man." She whirled around, gave Caitlan a quick kiss, and swished out, declaring dramatically as the door closed behind her, "Aristocratic knees, Garmon, I'd love to see the rest of you."

"You very nearly did," John Garmon yelled at the woman. He tugged at the robe and swore.

Caitlan Downey smothered a laugh. "Watch the language, Unc', little pitchers and all that."

Caity turned her head to follow the sound of John's voice and began to fuss.

"I'd fuss too," John observed dryly, "if I had a mother who spouted such inane nonsense. Unc'! It's never too early to talk honestly to a child."

"I'm sorry, darling," Caitlan said as she laid the child on the bed and reached for the diaper bag. "I'd like to explain to you why your uncle is wearing a lady's bathrobe and nothing else, but I'm afraid I don't know much about him yet. When you're a couple of weeks older, we'll discuss that kind of man."

"If you don't know me, it's not because your friends haven't done a full-scale examination of me, including someone who turned up at the crack of dawn to ogle me."

"Pay no attention, Caity. Mommie will change you while Uncle John takes off Mommie's robe and puts on his own clothes. We really don't mind that he's a little kinky, do we? After all, he's family."

"Kinky?" John groaned, his face flaming a light, but unmistakable, scarlet. "You're right, Caitlan. Wearing a lady's robe in front of my niece could give her an identity crisis. I'll just take it off and set the record straight."

Caitlan watched, spellbound, as John loosened the tie on the robe and shrugged his shoulders, allowing the skimpy garment to flutter majestically to the floor. Totally nude, he was magnificent, a true Viking—arrogant and angry.

Caitlan gasped.

John stood defiantly before her for a moment, picked up the robe, then strode past her into the living room.

"Danni's right," Caitlan called after him. "Very aristocratic knees, and the rest ain't too shabby either."

Nothing he could say would save the situation. John grabbed his satchel and headed for the kitchen, desperately pulling on his clothing before some other lost, curious, helpless soul wandered into Caitlan's home. For the first time ever, he was more interested in simply being dressed than in what he was wearing. He may have been more embarrassed at some point in his life, but he couldn't remember when. What had possessed him to strip in front of Caitlan and the baby? he asked himself. Less than twenty-four hours spent on the Carnival Strip and he'd become as uninhibited as the tourists.

He took a few calming deep breaths. Deep breathing didn't help. Concentrating on the ocean through the sliding glass doors didn't help either. In fact, the more he tried, the more angry he became. He'd behaved like a fool because he'd been caught in an embarrassing situation and hadn't known how to handle it. He wasn't an exhibitionist—at least not until recently.

The longer he paced in the kitchen the more foolish he felt. It was her fault, he decided. If she hadn't surprised him by arriving early, the incident never would have happened.

"How come you're home now?" Even to him his voice sounded peevish.

"Linda Brown came in early to return a favor I'd done for her last week. I told you I'd get home by myself."

"I know you can take care of yourself," John muttered under his breath. "If I didn't before, I've been told by Lieutenant Kelly, Tony the postman, and half the permanent population of the Carnival Strip."

By the time he'd prepared breakfast, he realized

that the bedroom had become silent. He walked across the thick carpet and looked in. Caitlan was sound asleep on the bed with the child curled in the curve of her arm.

Relaxed in sleep, Caitlan was even lovelier. Her pale, Dresden china complexion seemed at odds with her jet-black hair. Her dark eyes were closed, fanned by long, spiky black lashes, she looked like Sleeping Beauty waiting to be awakened with a kiss. She seemed fragile, in need of being cared for. But looks could be misleading, he realized. If there was a woman south of Atlanta who could look after herself, John Garmon knew he was staring at her.

At that moment the baby opened her dark eyes— Caitlan's dark eyes—and stared at John. She waited, as though she might be examining him, before she began to crinkle her lips. She was about to cry. She'd wake Caitlan who'd just worked two shifts. Without a thought John reached down and took the child. She quieted down when he lifted her. Caitlan shifted her body and slept on. John backed slowly from the room and closed the door behind him.

He would have put the child in her crib if she'd had one. John wracked his brain. What did one do with a baby, hold it all the time? He considered the situation scientifically. She obviously was too small to walk, she probably didn't crawl, so wherever she was placed was where she'd stay. Fine, he thought. He put her on the couch.

She cried.

John put her on Caitlan's robe on the carpet on the floor.

She cried again.

She seemed content to be held. But if he held the

child, he couldn't clear away the breakfast dishes. He couldn't even fix the cup of coffee he so desperately needed. His admiration for the mothers of the world—and Caitlan in particular—rose by startling degrees. Finally inspiration hit him. From a tablecloth he found in a cabinet, he fashioned a sling. By cutting a hole in the cloth, he could thread the child through it, wrap the remainder around her, and tie her to his chest like an Indian papoose in reverse. It worked very well. The baby was snug, he was mobile.

For the next two hours John Garmon took inventory of the house. The furnishings were fine, meager but fine. It was the absence of personal items that struck him. Caitlan's refrigerator wasn't well stocked. The cabinets were empty except for one can of formula, two bottles, baby vitamins, and three cans of soup. If Caitlan had been living on soup, it was no wonder she was so slender. From where he stood, she needed more substantial fare.

There was nothing for him to do but make another trip to the little store up the beach. But what would he do with the child? he wondered. Well, he thought, if the sling worked attached to him, it ought to work if he tied it to the bucket seat of his car. Luckily on his way out he spotted a car seat on the porch. Thirty minutes later he and Caity entered Willie's Grocery.

"Oh, it's little Caity, and you must be Garmon. It's about time!" The elderly man—Willie, John assumed—was sitting outside the old store, rocking back and forth as he absently swatted at flies. As John reached the steps the old man let out a stream of brown tobacco juice that narrowly missed John's bare leg.

"I suppose everybody on the Carnival Strip knows my name."

"Just about. What kept you?"

"It took me a while to find Caitlan. You can tell everyone that Caitlan ran away from home. I'm not the bad guy."

"She had good reason, I'm sure. Want me to hold Caity while you shop?" Willie held out his arms, and the child smiled at the dark-skinned old man who had two missing front teeth.

John reluctantly allowed the old man to take her. He was certain that Willie and Caity were acquainted, but he was surprised at how reluctant he was to release the baby. Quickly he covered the counter with enough food to last them several days. He was refused the use of his credit card.

"Only take green money, son. Just remember the amount and pay me later. Caitlan always does."

John drove back down the highway toward the cottage, shaking his head in disbelief. He unloaded the groceries and put them away, humming softly to himself and the child, whose eyelids were beginning to drift closed. This time when he tied her into her pouch, she placed her head on his shoulder. He could have put her down, but it felt good to hold her, and he didn't want to lose that feeling.

The unmistakable aroma of freshly brewed coffee nudged Caitlan awake. She sat up, taking in the smell of food cooking and the sound of movement inside her cottage.

Still half asleep, Caitlan looked around. Caity! She'd been in bed with her and now she was gone. Caitlan jumped to her feet, padded barefoot into the living room, then stopped. The patio doors were open. Beyond the redwood deck a peaceful turquoise-blue ocean blended into the clear blue sky. She watched in amazement as the breeze ruffled a bright yellow tablecloth draped across the round table.

Not only was there a platter of ground beef patties on the table, but there was also a glass bowl filled with crisp lettuce, cucumbers, and tomatoes. The light inside the microwave oven displayed a loaf of French bread turning around and around on the carousel.

"Darn, sweetheart, we forgot to get butter."

"Butter?" Caitlan's breath whooshed out of her lungs in an explosion of relief. "Sweetheart?"

"Sorry, Caitlan. Caity and I should have picked up some at the market, but with Willie carrying on a nonstop tirade on my callous treatment of you and this child, I guess I forgot." John rose from the squatting position he'd assumed to examine the sparse contents of the refrigerator.

"We? You took my baby to the store with you?"

"Correction, ma'am, I took 'our' baby to the store."

"Caity isn't your baby and what are you doing?"

"I'm making lunch. Correction, Caity and I are making lunch. Uh-oh! Shush! I think we've lost Dumplin'."

The child had fallen forward onto John's chest and was sleeping soundly.

Caitlan couldn't take her eyes off John and Caity. He looked so ridiculous with a baby tied to his chest. Yet he looked natural at the same time. He wasn't embarrassed like other men might have been. Nothing about the man she was looking at fit with the picture of him she'd formed in her mind. Chairman of the Board? Most eligible bachelor in Savannah, Georgia? She didn't know what he was, but none of those tags seemed to fit.

"If I could find her bed, I'd put her down," he said with a glance at the sleeping child, a glance that was so tender, Caitlan felt her resistance begin to melt away. "I assume that babies still take naps?"

"Yes, of course they do." Caitlan blinked her eyes. Maybe she was half asleep after the long shift she'd just worked. Of course Caity loved everybody, but John Garmon? she hadn't expected that.

"Here, I'll take her." Caitlan lifted her from the cotton sling that John had concocted and took her into the bedroom. She pulled out the bottom bureau drawer and laid her inside.

"I should have known," John observed wryly from the doorway. "But I didn't dare risk plundering in your drawers. Sorry, bad pun."

He stood in the doorway, his lips curved into a smile, his eyes almost the same color as the sea behind him. A faded pair of cutoff jeans replaced the carefully fitted linen trousers he'd been wearing the night before. The jeans covered his slim hips like a second skin. He, too, was barefoot. For a long moment he waited, then with a sweep of his hand and a click of his heels he bowed low. "Madam, would you care to join me on the deck for some lunch? Caity and I prepared it just for you."

"No. Yes . . . Let me take off this uniform and jump under the shower, and I'll be right out."

She whirled around and into the bathroom, closing the door behind her.

"Wait," John started to say, remembering that her

robe was back in the kitchen where he'd left it. But she couldn't hear him with the water running.

John stopped to look at the baby sleeping quietly in the bureau drawer, then headed for the kitchen, intent on returning Caitlan's robe to her. She was telling the truth when she said she was going to jump under the shower, he learned as he stepped back into the bedroom with her robe. She was wrapped in a beach towel that had psychedelic pink flamingos on its black background.

"Oh!"

"Sorry." They both spoke at the same time.

"That towel is pretty spectacular," John finally said, holding out the robe. It wasn't the towel that was spectacular, and he well knew it. It was the woman who brought a zing to his pulse.

"It belonged to a friend," Caitlan answered, motionless before him.

"I borrowed your robe earlier."

"I know, I saw you. Aristocratic knees, remember?"

"Mine are nothing to compare with yours."

A hard lump had lodged itself in her throat. She didn't want to get close to John Garmon. Every time she looked at him, she felt as if she were spinning like the pinwheels Racer Malone sold from his souvenir cart down on the beach.

"Please, Mr. Garmon . . ."

"John," he corrected softly. "We can't seem to keep our clothes on around each other, can we?"

"I'd like to get dressed now," she said.

Her hair wasn't wet, but beads of water rolled down her exposed arm. Her lips were parted in agitation, which was made even plainer by the rapid movement of her breasts as she breathed.

"Please . . . John?"

"Oh, sorry. Yes. I'll have our lunch ready on the deck." He turned and gave her a clear view of his aristocratic legs.

John Garmon was a disturbing man, and after a long shift Caitlan's equilibrium was rocky at best. He was too attractive, too in charge, and much, much too appealing. And there she was, knowing how dangerous he was proving to be, and all she wanted to do was stare at him.

Quickly she pulled on a loose-fitting pink dress, took the pins out of her hair, tied it back with a pink ribbon, and headed to the kitchen.

"I'm sure you know that sunshine is a major source of vitamin D," he said. "As long as it's taken in small amounts, the body absorbs the vitamins much like the vitamin C in orange juice."

"I know," she agreed as she joined him on the deck. She leaned on the rail overlooking the brilliant white beach. "I'm a nurse."

"Well, I'm no expert, mind you, but I'd say from the looks of you that your body is crying out for A and D. Don't you hear it?"

"A and D?" She glanced at him in confusion. It was a mistake. He was too close, too masculine. "What?" she asked.

"Vitamin D, remember?" He smiled.

His smile startled her and she blushed. She focused her eyes on the redwood deck, wondering how in heaven's name she was going to resist the man who seemed to have moved into her life. She hadn't expected her life to be easy, but with John Garmon there, her future plans could be in big trouble.

"Sit down." John walked over and sat down at the redwood table, patting the seat beside him. "Eat.

Nutritious food and natural vitamins makes babies grow strong and healthy, and strengthens your bones and teeth."

"Like yours?" The words shot out before she realized that she'd even thought them.

"I'm not nursing a baby, but I'm glad to know that you've checked out my teeth. I thought you had some kind of knee fetish."

Caitlan looked puzzled.

"Your eyes seemed permanently grounded. You've looked everywhere except at me. If you don't sit down, I'm going to have to get my rope and tie you to the chair. Lunch is getting cold."

"You wouldn't dare." She couldn't tell whether he was joking or not. Something about his voice suggested he might be serious, and short of actually getting Kelly to throw him out which she wouldn't do anyway, she couldn't think of any logical way to stop him. "Maybe I'll have a cup of that great-smelling coffee."

"Suit yourself," he answered, taking a large forkful of lettuce and chewing lustily, "but my ma would be stiff-lipped and put out if I refused to eat after somebody went to the trouble of preparing food for me."

"Your mother would snap her corset if she ever heard you call her ma. I saw the legendary Mettie Garmon at the funeral, remember? Black designer suit, pearls, silver hair, and all. I'm sure she sent you to poison me, not feed me," Caitlan observed shrewdly and flopped down in the chair across the table.

"We considered that," he admitted honestly, "but Jeffrey asked us . . . me," he corrected, "to look after you, and that's what I'm going to do. Cooking for you is my own idea. It's one thing I know I can do. Are you always so grouchy in the morning?"

"No," she answered honestly. "I'm rarely ever grouchy. I guess it's just the strain of having you here." Caitlan took a sip of coffee. "Mmmm, this is very good."

"And so is this." He picked up his fork, jabbed it into a meat patty and held it against her lips until she took the food. "Cooking is just one of my talents."

Caitlan chewed and swallowed hard. "In addition to having aristocratic body parts? You're a remarkable man, John Garmon, when you take off your mask."

"Sure, I'm a good guy once you get to know me."

"Just like Gene Autry," Caitlan said, accepting another bite of meat.

"Gene Autry? You mean the man who owns the baseball team?"

Caitlan chuckled. "I can see there is a glaring void in your education, Mr. Corporate Executive. It's positively un-American. Yes, Mr. Autry owns a baseball team, but didn't you ever watch any of his old western movies on television?"

"No, I haven't. Reading an occasional Lone Ranger comic book as a kid is about as western as I ever got."

Caitlan pushed his fork away and took another sip of coffee. "I wasn't even born when Gene Autry made his films, but old western movies are my hobby. Gene and Roy Rogers were always the guys that came to the rescue of the lady in distress. Afterward they serenaded her as they rode off into the sunset."

"Ah, too bad. You worked right through the sunset I rode off into."

"Shucks!" she said, joining in the lighthearted repartee. "And I missed your serenade too."

"Maybe you ought to be glad about that."

Caitlan laughed. The man was really outrageous. She was enjoying herself and she hadn't expected to.

"Oh, dear," John observed in mock horror. "I finally got you to smile, and here it comes again—the 'I'm not sure I trust him' look."

"Of course I trust you, John. Why shouldn't I?"

Why shouldn't she? He couldn't delay it any longer. He might just as well get it out into the open. "Because I came to take back your inheritance."

"Oh, I expected you to. I'll cooperate, if that's what's bugging you," she said, a quizzical look on her face.

Dammit, he thought, he almost believed she really wasn't aware of what she'd said, but he had to go through with it. "You must not know the extent of your windfall."

Caitlan stood and walked to the deck rail, turning her back to John Garmon. She had to listen to what he had to say, but she didn't want to watch him as he spoke. He was too distracting.

"What do you mean?" she asked quietly. She'd been afraid that the family would somehow manage to find out her secret. She'd left Pretty Springs after the funeral for that reason. She never expected that Jeffrey himself would give the secret away, and she dreaded hearing what John was about to reveal. Avoiding the issue wouldn't work. She might as well hear it all. "I guess I don't. Tell me."

John joined her, leaning his hands on the rail. "He left you the farm."

"He did?"

"Yes, but after checking into it I found out that he paid too much for the land. The interest is too high and it's unlikely that you'll be able to sell it without taking a loss. The bottom line is that you won't make money on it."

"Fine, give it away."

"That isn't all." John ignored her flippant comment. It was obvious he didn't want to talk about the rest, but he'd been right when he said he accepted his responsibilities and fulfilled his obligations. He'd do whatever he'd been asked to do, but he didn't have to look at her while he did it. "Are you familiar with the company?"

"You mean the Garmon Chocolate Company? Yes, but what does that have to do with me?"

"Jeffrey left you one thousand shares of stock in Garmon Chocolate, one third of the company in the event of both his and Ann's deaths.

Caitlan gasped. "One third of the company? I didn't know." She turned and walked a few steps.

"Well, now you do. But now that I know about Caity, that she is his heir, it changes what I had decided to do."

Caitlan turned to face the man standing behind her. "You mean I would have a say in the operation of the company?" She couldn't conceal a smile at his distress.

"Yes, legally you would. But we wouldn't expect you to be concerned with the company's operations."

"Oh, but I am. I most definitely have my own ideas about the Garmon Chocolate Company. There is one change I'd like you to make right away." She put a stern expression on her face.

"There is?"

"Yes, I'd like it if you'd make a really gooey, sweet, sticky, chocolate-covered cherry," she said in a teasing voice, and caught his hand in an exaggerated plea. "Could we do that, partner?"

"Chocolate-covered cherries? That's all you want?"

"Yes, otherwise Garmon Chocolates are just about perfect. Relax, John, I don't want your company. I'll sign over any control I might have."

"But . . ."

"For myself," she went on without giving him time to argue, "I'd refuse the stock completely, but I have to think of Caity, and I'll keep ownership for her until she grows up. Then she can make her own decisions. In the meantime, you go ahead and vote my shares. I'll look after Caity and myself. I always have."

It took a moment for her answer to sink in and another few seconds for him to determine that she was serious. Foolishly he realized that he'd been towering over her like a schoolteacher threatening the maker of a spitball, and she was holding his hand as if she'd forgotten about it.

"Well, that's a relief," he said lightly, wiping an imaginary line of sweat from his forehead. "But it isn't that easy. I have a duty to the company and to my brother. He sent me to see that you and the baby were provided for, and I have to do that, one way or another."

"Ah, John, you'd never qualify as a real cowboy on a white horse. You're too serious. I don't think you'd even make a good outlaw—you have no imagination."

"Maybe I don't have much imagination," he admitted sharply, "but there are a lot of things I do well, Caitlan Downey. And if you'll let me, I'll show you, beginning with the baby. She needs a real bed. I intend to buy one tomorrow."

Caitlan bit back a protest, looked down, and, realizing she was squeezing his hand, let it go. After all, Caity was John Garmon's niece. Letting him buy a crib wasn't handing over control of the child's life. The gift was reasonable.

"All right, John, but we really aren't your responsibility. What would your mother say if she could see you now? Does she know about Caity?"

"No, not yet. I wanted to see you first." John looked at Caitlan for a long moment. She'd asked a good question, one he wasn't sure he wanted to answer. "I'm my own man, Caitlan, in spite of what my brother may have told you. I plead guilty to following all the rules. I respect my mother's wishes and wash behind my ears."

"And you have aristocratic knees too." Caitlan grinned, moving back to the table. The sun was too bright. She needed the shelter of the beach umbrella, and she needed to put the distance of the table between them.

"I wish you'd talk to me, Caitlan. Why did you agree to have my brother's child. It can't have been an easy decision."

"I agreed because Ann couldn't conceive. And if you don't mind, John, I don't want to talk about Jeffrey and Ann and me. We had a special, private relationship. You're asking personal questions that even my closest friends wouldn't ask. Let's drop the subject, shall we?"

"I find it hard to believe that your friends didn't ask about your past. There seems to be precious little about you that they don't know."

"Oh, they know. I told them, or at least I told them part of the truth."

"Fine, suppose you tell me."

"I've told you all you need to know."

"I have a right to know the circumstances. Jeffrey was my brother, dammit! And it was quite a shock to find out he had a child."

"Caity is Jeffrey's biological daughter," Caitlan said. "Now that he's gone, she's my child—just mine."

"I find all that very hard to understand." John knew that he was pushing her. She was tired, but even after working part of an extra shift she was still beautiful. Her dark hair blowing in the light breeze, expressive eyes gazing at him with undisguised emotion, all brought a faint sense of frustration to him. He would not permit himself to be attracted to her. There already were too many complications. But he knew that Caity bound them together, no matter what either of them thought.

"You don't have to do anything. We're not talking about profit and loss decisions. We're talking about a child, a tiny baby. This baby was planned, she's an expression of love, a gift from me to the two people in the world that I loved most. I don't expect you to understand. I don't even know why I'm discussing it with you. Go away, John Garmon!"

She boldly met his gaze, trying desperately to conceal the panic that simmered just below the surface of her control. Damn! She hadn't meant to let him force her into an admission of her situation. She pressed her hand against her forehead and grimaced. She was so tired. Moisture collected in her eyes. Lord, she thought, she was about to cry. She, Caitlan Downey who never cried, felt tears running down her cheeks in a river. What was wrong with her?

In an instant John Garmon was beside her, drawing her into his embrace as naturally as if he'd done it a hundred times. "Shhh, I'm sorry Caitlan." He pressed her face into his shoulder, patting her back absently until she began to relax. "I didn't mean to upset you. You just seem so calm about your situation."

"I made my choice and I don't regret it. I just didn't expect to have to care for her alone," she whispered in a low voice. His arms felt good. She'd known they would. She'd been embraced in them once before at the Garmon house the night after the funeral. For weeks afterward she'd remembered being in those arms. Then gradually she'd managed to put him out of her mind. Now he was holding her again and it felt very, very right.

"You aren't alone now, Caitlan. No more arguing. No more questions. We'll work it out. We'll call a truce, get to know each other, and then we'll decide together what's to be done. Everything is okay." He nuzzled her hair with his lips the same way he'd comforted the child when she'd cried. But it was different. When Caitlan lifted her eyes and looked up at him, what he saw in her eyes was need. And he knew that her need was only a reflection of his own.

The blood pounded in his veins. He didn't intend to kiss her—but he did.

She didn't intend to kiss him back—but she couldn't stop herself.

The warm, firm feeling of his lips on hers was an unexpected sensation that confused her. For a moment she lost herself in the knowledge that he found her desirable as a woman. The unmistakable, hot, shivery sensation of his touch ignited her skin.

She felt his shudder of response as she raised

herself on tiptoe to put her arms around his neck. She hadn't counted on this melting together, on being fused like two pieces of glass heated by the blue-white torch of a glass blower. None of the kisses she'd shared up to now in any way prepared her for the overwhelming sensations that raced through her body. He was so big and strong.

The kiss was urgent, rough, and frantic. Great waves of desire swept over them like the frantic rush of the incoming tide at the water's edge.

Lordy, how she wanted this man, she thought.

Damn, how he wanted this woman, he thought. She pushed every reasonable thought from his mind, and he changed into a man with a need beyond duty and family. Caitlan was everything missing in his life. She was joy and wonder, and he wanted to protect and cherish her—no matter what had happened before.

"Please! Please, John," she whispered incoherently.

He stiffened and pulled back, seeing new tears glinting in her dark eyes.

"Ah, Caitlan, what have I done?"

"You?" Her confusion was as great as his. "I let you do it."

She'd been wrong. John Garmon *was* the enemy, and she'd not only waved the white flag, she'd wrapped herself up in it and declared her surrender.

Three

Caitlan met Tony at the door just as he was slipping a circular into the mailbox. "Morning, Tony."

"Morning, Caitlan. Met your man yesterday."

"I heard."

" 'Bout time he got here. A woman's got no business raising a child alone when the baby has a perfectly good father."

"But the baby isn't—" she cut her words short. What did it matter? Saying that the baby wasn't John's would only complicate things. After all, she reasoned for the hundredth time since she'd pulled herself from his arms, John would only be around long enough to work out the details of the stock transfer. Then he'd be gone, and she could get her life organized again.

She'd been grateful that John had stopped kissing her and backed away. She couldn't—wouldn't—have stopped him otherwise. He'd been as disturbed by their kiss as she had been. Soon afterward he changed his clothes and announced that he was going into town to run a few errands. He didn't ask her to go, which was just as well. Being closed up with him again in his car with the darkened windows would have been too much of a temptation.

Caitlan's head began to pound. She told Tony goodbye and went back inside. She really was very tired. Maybe she'd take a nap while Caity was asleep. She punched up her pillow, pulled the sheet over her, and closed her eyes. He was not the Lone Ranger, she decided, nor was he an outlaw. It was she who felt like the criminal. Owning stock in the Garmon Chocolate Company wasn't for her. She was a simple person. But Caity, she was a different story. Caity was a Garmon, and she'd keep the stock for her, even if that decision did make her feel like a crook.

John Garmon was a cross between Luke Skywalker and Casanova—stern and filled with moral righteousness, charging in to rescue her one minute whether she wanted to be rescued or not, then kissing her senseless the next.

She liked the idea of the young Jedi warrior, but the wildly passionate experienced lover was intoxicating too. In truth, she was more comfortable with her Gene Autry and Roy Rogers movies. The bad guys were always bad and the good guys always won. Simple, that's the way she liked her life, the way it had been before John Garmon arrived.

When the television set arrived at one-thirty, the groceries at two o'clock, and the baby furniture at three, Caitlan knew that her Jedi warrior was on the move again. But it was the arrival of a locksmith to change the locks and supply new keys that told her what it really meant to cope with Garmon take-charge power. She'd have to explain to John that the cottage wasn't hers and that she had a television —though she'd loaned it to the Winslows.

She'd also have to explain that when she'd approved a crib she hadn't expected a frosty white creation with a crocheted lace canopy and baby bears on the headboard. The matching chests, rocking chair, playpen, and high chair definitely weren't on the approved list.

By late afternoon she'd bathed, fed, and dressed Caity. Then she'd showered and changed into a loose-fitting cherry-colored sundress with spaghetti straps and a long skirt that flowed below her knees. For an hour she'd alternated between being glad that John Garmon had left her alone and wondering nervously when he'd be back. Finally, taking Caity in her arms, she started off down the beach for a walk to calm her nerves.

From the side of the highway above, John Garmon stood by the Blazer he'd bought in Caitlan's name and watched her walk along the water's edge. She intrigued him. The moment he'd realized she was pregnant at the funeral he'd been puzzled. Jeffrey's note had only added to his fascination. What kind of woman bore her brother-in-law's child with her sister's approval? One who worked part of an extra shift when she already was dead-tired so that a co-worker could attend her child's college graduation. One who had her telephone bill paid by a friend who didn't want to worry that a child might need help. A special kind of woman, he decided, who was driving him crazy even when he was away from her. He cursed his own weakness and started down the dune toward her. Nothing he'd found out along the Strip had changed the picture of Caitlan Downey that he'd been presented with. She was a genuinely good person, well liked, and generous to a fault.

In short, Caitlan was a lot like Jeffrey—and she was John's chance to make things right. He deeply regretted never having reached out to his brother. He hadn't known how. Running corporations was a snap, but making personal compromises was harder. Caitlan was his second chance. Before he left Florida he intended to mend fences and develop a real relationship with the mother of his brother's child. He'd start with dinner.

The noisy seafood restaurant was filled with young couples and the sound of country music. John watched Caitlan as she spoke to one friend and waved to another. She simply introduced him to her friends as John, and they accepted him without question. She couldn't know how relaxed and warm she looked in the soft candlelight.

"This is nice, John."

"I'm sorry. What did you say? The music is very loud, and sad."

"Sad? Cowboy lesson number two, John. Cowboys like sad songs. That's Randy Travis's new she-done-me-wrong hit tune."

"I believe it—the she-done-me-wrong part anyway. Who's Randy Travis?"

"There are some serious gaps in your education.

Randy Travis is the country singer of the year. Surely you've heard him?"

"I don't think so," he admitted, more involved in noting the air of warmth and relaxation about the woman across from him.

"I'll bet you know all the operas and can recognize most classical pieces."

"Well, yes," he said, feeling out of step with his present surroundings. "The family does have a box at the opera."

"Thought so." She grinned. "Well, listen up, John. Randy Travis was the entertainer of the year and this song sold a million copies. Though the songs in my favorite western movies, the ones I know so well, lean more toward subjects such as herding cows and finding water. You take the Sons of the Pioneers, they were a band!"

John never imagined he'd ever listen to a country-music song, but he had to admit that the tune had a certain appeal. But he couldn't be sure whether it was the music or the woman extolling its merits that gave him a different point of view. "It does sound like a good tune to dance to."

Her smile brightened as she caught his hand and pulled him swiftly to his feet. "I think I'll just show you how much fun it can be. Come on, cowboy."

"Oh, I don't know whether I can dance or not, Ms. Downey, ma'am. I've been accused of having two left feet."

"With those aristocratic knees? I doubt it. All you have to do is hold me."

"Now that's a plan I can relate to."

There was a postage-sized dance floor in front of the band already packed with energetic dancers.

Caitlan pulled John into the crowd and looped his arms loosely around her. Quickly he followed the motions of the other dancers and shuffled her slowly around the floor. That he had no idea what he was doing didn't seem to matter as they didn't have enough room to follow any special steps. It was simply a matter of keeping to the rhythm. At first he tried to avoid body contact, but Caitlan wouldn't comply.

"What's the matter, John?"

"What?" He leaned down to hear what she was saying.

"That's better." She twined her arms behind his neck and buried her forehead under his chin. They moved more and more slowly as the music grew slower and sadder. Caitlan seemed to melt against him, filling the hollows of his body as if she'd been poured into his mold. One tune gave way to another, and John lost track of where they were as his hands began to range intimately across her lower back.

The crowd faded away and there was only the two of them and the music, sad music about broken hearts and good loving. Caitlan was wonderfully feminine, totally beautiful, and John had never felt so fulfilled. The music came to an end and a hush fell over the crowd. In that moment of silence, there was an unmistakable growl from Caitlan's stomach that sounded like the muted roar of fans at a college football game.

"I guess you're hungry." He grinned, reluctant to release her.

"Not me," Caitlan said dreamily, "it's my stomach."

John adjusted his position and pulled her closer.

"Not bad dancing for a beginner, Mr. Garmon, sir. In fact, it could be said that your Texas two-step was awesome."

Awesome might not be a good name for what his attempt at the Texas two-step had accomplished, but it was an accurate assessment of his reaction to the tiny woman looking up at him with laughter in her eyes.

John turned her around and walked her to the table, pressing close to her as they walked. He was glad that the waitress was there filling quart-sized mason jars with iced tea as they reached the table. He needed the interruption to compose himself. He was coming to the disturbing realization that this wasn't just a simple "getting to know you" game he'd embarked on. Mended fences might turn out to corral the mender instead of the renegade.

"What'll you folks have?" the waitress asked.

"John?"

"You order for me, Caitlan. I'm like a fish out of water, no pun intended."

"Apt statement in a fish house, Luke."

He pulled her into the booth and slid in beside her, ignoring the place setting on the opposite side of the table.

"Luke?"

"Sorry, slip of the tongue. Bring boiled shrimp— lots of boiled shrimp—and hot sauce," Caitlan directed.

John gave a nod of agreement, dismissed the waitress, and turned back to Caitlan. "Are you okay?"

"At this point that's a question I don't think I want to answer. How'd you arrange for Danni to keep Caity so we could spend this evening on the town?"

"It didn't take but one step to find out where Danni Manderson lived and two steps to corner her with my proposal. She's a very interesting person, your friend Danni. She's taking our child to her consciousness-raising class. Is she always so dramatic?"

"Always. Danni has a theory that life is too short and too dull. If she can dress it up, why not do so?"

"Well, the dumplin' seems to like her. Though in all honesty, I think the kid likes everybody. What did you do while I was away today?"

"Well . . ." She found it hard to speak when he was so close. Inching away, she felt the hard slab of log wall against her arm. "The television set, the groceries, and the baby furniture were delivered. After that the locksmith came, but you know all that."

"Good."

"Not good. I said you could get a bed, not a warehouse full of furniture."

"I know, but I couldn't resist the bears. Dumpling will love the pink and blue bears on the bed, and little girls ought to have lace around them, oughtn't they?"

He was so enthusiastic that she didn't have the heart to reprimand him further. Caity had that effect on people. Why should her uncle be different? "All right, but you shouldn't have had the locks changed, John. I don't own the cottage. The owner could be very upset about it."

"I have it on good authority that the owner won't mind," John assured her. He could tell her that he'd bought the cottage, but he didn't want to scare her off and defeat his whole purpose in providing for her future. The more he could do for her, the more comfortable he'd feel about his mission, he told himself. "With everybody on the Gulf Coast marching in and out, I'd like to know that you'll be safe."

"But I'm very safe. Tony the postman checks on me every morning, and Kelly brings me home from work on the nights I work late. There's Danni and Jeb. I'm fine—really."

She looked fine. With a flush of pink in her cheeks and her eyes shining in the half-light, John felt a surge of some emotion he couldn't identify. It wouldn't be pushed away. He leaned close. She didn't move. Damn, he wanted to kiss her again. The waitress brought their food, interrupting the mood. He watched intently as she placed a large platter of boiled shrimp in the center of the table.

"So," Caitlan said as she began to peel a fat pink shrimp with her fingers, "what did you do this afternoon while you were away?"

"Aside from the furniture, I bought the Blazer, swimming trunks, some shorts, and—a robe."

"Ah, and you looked so cute in mine."

"Cute is not a word for a man on a rescue mission."

"True. You must be the only man in the world who goes into town and casually buys a four-wheel-drive vehicle the day after you've come in a forty-thousand-dollar car. Why did you do it?"

"I don't want you hitchhiking anymore, Caitlan. It isn't safe. You seemed uncomfortable in my car, so I bought the Blazer for you."

"You bought the Blazer for me? Do you do this sort of thing often?"

"Absolutely never. It must be you. You make me do crazy things. I'm not normally a spur-of-the-moment kind of person." He took a large boiled shrimp, peeled away the shell, and submerged it in the thick red sauce. "I make lots of plans. Do you?"

"Not usually. At least not until now." Caitlan became very interested in the shrimp. She chewed lustily. A spot of sauce dribbled down her chin, and she laughed as John caught it with his napkin. "Messy, isn't it?" She finished the shrimp and started on another. "What kind of plans have you made?"

"Well, you can't go on house-sitting and working part-time. The child needs more stability than that. What about marriage?"

"What?" She let out a startled breath. "Are you proposing?"

"No, I meant . . ." he faltered, "do you have plans to marry in the future? Your friend Danni said lots of interested men had asked you out and you'd turned them all down. I'd like to meet the man first, because of Caity, but marriage is a good idea. I think a child needs a father."

"I see. You've got everything worked out, haven't you? Buy us everything we need, find a man to look after us, and then you're out of here." Caitlan gave a derisive snort. "You'd be fulfilling your brother's request, and you'd be off the hook. Not bad list making, John—very well planned."

John looked at Caitlan in amazement. She actually was nodding in agreement. He'd been sure that she'd fight him all the way.

"This place is something, isn't it?" He'd thought she was agreeing with his plan. She wasn't. She was simply too angry to honor it with a discussion. "I've never been here before. It's hard to believe how crowded it is."

"You must know half the people here. How come they're not descending on you like they do at the cottage?"

"Because they think we want to be alone. I'd better tell you, John," she said sweetly, "before you decide to advertise for a husband for me, they think you're Caity's father. So, none of the men are likely to present themselves for your approval as a candidate. I guess it's just you and me, kid."

"They think I'm the father? Why?"

"Because of Caity's birth certificate. She's listed as Caitlan Ann Garmon. Those things get around. When you showed up and gave your name to Tony as Garmon, that's all it took. This is fun, isn't it, darling?" Caitlan patted his cheek and stifled a grin at the shocked expression on his face.

"No wonder they were ready to tar and feather me. And when I leave, they'll probably send that posse you're always talking about to bring me in for some old-fashioned western justice."

"Could be. Floridians are very moral people."

"So are Georgians, darling." Two could play her game. John caught Caitlan's hand and kissed her fingertips lovingly, suggestively. "They're good lovers too."

Caitlan gasped and brought her teasing to an end. She hadn't meant to alarm him. He'd been so bossy with his planning that she couldn't resist shooting holes in his neat and tidy plan. Her teasing seemed to backfire as all her other great pronouncements had done since John stepped into the picture. She took a long sip of tea.

"There was a time," she said, "when I would have been the one tarred and feathered, being here with you. My mama would have my bottom bare in a minute."

Given a new target of attack, John rose to the occasion. "Why? Why would anyone have reason to attack you?"

"Mama didn't approve of sad music and close dancing." Caitlan's voice went lower, and John had to strain to catch her words. "There wasn't much about men that Mama did approve of—women either, for that matter."

"Pretty tough on you, was she?"

"Yes. 'Caitlan Downey!' she'd yell with both hands on her hips, 'you get out there in that yard and bring me a switch from that peach tree and shuck those pants, pronto.'"

"Shuck those pants?" John laughed. "I know it's not funny to you, but I've never heard such expressions. Where are you from?"

"About twenty miles south of here, a little town that dried up and blew away ten years before I was born. I graduated from the consolidated county high school not far from the Strip. That's why all those people look after me. I've known them all my life."

"My mother left, but she didn't have anywhere to go and no ambition to find a place."

"And shuck your pants?" he prompted. "You mean she beat you?"

"Beat? Not my mama. She never beat anybody in her life. She just gave a switching that cut your legs and made you so sore, you couldn't walk for days. She had her own way of reminding Ann and me that we were expected to behave ourselves."

"And did you?" John couldn't miss the fleeting look of pain in her face as he realized how little he knew about her.

"For a long time we did. But Mama became more and more pious. We were sinners of the worst kind, according to Mama. Then the switchings got worse and she traded her switch for a belt. One day we left. Ann and I were old enough so she couldn't bring us back. And then she died, and we could never go back. It bothered Ann a lot. Jeffrey used to hold her and let her cry. He used to . . . well, that's all over. All of them are gone now," she said solemnly, and changed the subject.

They talked about Atlanta as they ate, about places they'd both been and incidents they recalled. Finally they were down to the last shrimp on the plate. Caitlan looked at it for a long moment and then shook her head in refusal. "Are you done?"

"Overdone," John admitted, pleasantly stuffed.

"Dessert?"

"No way," John said with a groan. "Just roll me to the door. I'd say we both met our vitamin quotas today."

They paid the bill and strolled outside into the clear night air.

"So, tell me about your family," she said as he drove the shiny new Blazer back down the beach highway.

"Well, there's not much to tell, Cait. Your life has been a lot more eventful than mine."

"My life? 'Fraid not. I'm really a pretty ordinary person."

"No," he said softly, finding her hand in the darkness, "I don't believe there is anything ordinary about

Caitlan Downey. And I want to know all about her. I want very much to know."

"Only if you do the same by telling me all about you." Caitlan felt a warm sense of camaraderie begin between them and she responded by sliding closer to him and laying her hand on his shoulder as he shifted gears.

"All right," he agreed solemnly, "I'll tell you all about myself on the way home."

John stopped at the tollbooth and dropped in the fare, then drove across the long bridge that spanned the bay. There was a crisp breeze blowing through the open windows and the music on the radio was soft and intimate.

"Here comes the Garmon family saga. There were only two of us, Jeffrey was the older. Five years later I was born. Our father was a hale and hearty marine. I never really knew him. He was killed in an obscure accident while he was on peace patrol in Lebanon for the U.N."

"And your mother?"

"Ah, yes. Matilda Ellen, Mettie. My father married her, made her a vice president of Garmon Chocolate, and went off to the Korean War. He never was much good at business, but Mettie was a natural. I think that's why he married her. It's Mother who has the brains to run the show—Mother, and to some extent me. We're the only ones who've taken an active part in the company. Jeffrey refused any income at all, though as you know he owned a third of the company."

"Grandparents?"

"They're deceased," he said. "You?"

"None."

"Caitlan . . ." He hesitated for a moment then continued seriously, "Wasn't there anybody to see you through the pregnancy?"

She turned in the darkness to look at him. Why shouldn't he ask about her family? After all, she'd already told him more than she'd ever told anybody.

"Nope."

"Not even a maiden aunt stashed away somewhere ready to drive you crazy?" John didn't know why he kept asking. The more he found out, the more he was bothered. She evoked something paternal in him, but that was to be expected, he kept reminding himself. He was there to be the caretaker. It was his other feelings for her that he kept pushing away.

"Not a one. How about you? Isn't there a lady or two you're passionately in love with?"

"Not now, not ever. I'm a confirmed bachelor. What about you," he asked casually, "ever been in love?"

Even when he wasn't looking at her he could see her dark eyes fringed with thick lashes and swimming with emotion. He'd never been a man to hold back before. If a woman interested him, he said so, and more times than not the interest was reciprocated. Never before had his interest been centered on a woman with a child, however. But little Caity wasn't just any child, he remembered, she was Jeffrey's child.

The good citizens on the Carnival Strip didn't know about Jeffrey. They believed the child was his. He'd never thought about having a child before. Until Caity, he'd never even held one. John shook off the crazy feelings he'd experienced ever since Caitlan had told him that the world thought he was the father. He forced his mind not to examine the picture that it conjured up. He and Caitlan . . . no!

His thoughts went too far. The more he was around her, the more he knew that walking away was going to be almost impossible. Ruthless, be ruthless, John, he kept reminding himself. Don't get so emotionally involved. You can't want this woman. There are too many complications. He gripped the steering wheel even tighter as he waited for Caitlan's reply.

"No," Caitlan answered quietly. "I've never been in love. There is no man in my life, not anymore. Ann and I were alone until she married Jeff. Now, they're gone. That's the way it has to be."

Not anymore, she'd said, but she'd also said that she'd never been in love. A knot of tension wrenched his gut, and he let out a deep breath of air.

They drove along the edge of the beach. The long empty ribbon of white sand echoed the sloshing sounds of the ocean across the dunes and into the car.

Caitlan had known when she fled to the Gulf Coast that she wouldn't be able to hide forever. She'd known when Caity was born that her life would change. She just hadn't known the change would bring John Garmon. Now he was there. Of course he was overbearing, overwhelming even. But in spite of everything, he was nice. He was sweet, silly, and he felt like anything but a brother to her. At the moment, she didn't care.

They stopped by Danni's house and reclaimed the sleeping baby. John carried Caity's diaper bag and tipped Danni generously, pretending not to hear her suggestion that he dump Caitlan and the kid and come back after sundown. The sun had been down for hours, though the moon hadn't topped the trees in the distance. Caitlan fed the baby in the darkness as they drove home. They didn't speak, and the silence became louder than words.

The cottage was dark. John took her arm and helped her up the steps and inside, opening the door with a key he had already attached to his ring. Caity didn't stir as Caitlan laid her in her new crib.

Caitlan stood looking down at her for a long time. Was she right in making the decisions she'd made? Would Caity be better off back in Savannah with the Garmons? No! She would never go back on her word to Jeffrey and Ann. Giving up the child would have destroyed her. Caity was hers and she'd never let her go.

Caitlan walked into the living room. She stood looking through the window into the night. The heartbeat of the tide mingled with her own racing pulse, and she felt the humming begin in the tips of her toes.

"Good night, Caitlan. I enjoyed the evening. I even enjoyed the cowboy songs."

He was standing behind her. She turned, the darkness hiding the growing emotion she couldn't conceal. "Good night, John. Do you need anything?" She smiled up at him, her eyes shimmering.

John forced himself to think of shrimp, of Caity, of chocolate-covered cherries, anything but the woman staring at him with stars in her eyes. He wouldn't think of her lips, half parted in anticipation, of how much he wanted to claim them, taste them, feel her body pliant against him.

She was so beautiful, so trusting, and she wanted him too. Even if she didn't know it, he could tell.

Why not? Why not make love to her? The world thought he already had. He was aching for her. One of the straps on her sundress had slipped down on her shoulder and he could see the swell of her breast. Her nipples were hard, full, and inviting, and he wanted . . .

John groaned. "Oh, yes, you Western witch, you're making an outlaw out of me. . . ."

He leaned down.

She stood on her tiptoes.

"No," he said, then his voice became husky and he amended his dishonest answer. "Yes, I need you, Caitlan Downey. I need you very much."

"I know," was her only answer.

Their lips met and she was in his arms, pressing herself against him. The straps of her dress slipped further down her arms, her breasts were bared. She moaned as he filled his hands with their fullness.

Tides of passion rocked John Garmon. He felt as though he'd been caught in the current and tossed against the rocks. The woman parting her lips hesitantly beneath his was trembling as she caught the back of his head with her hands and held him tight.

"Oh, hell, Caitlan," he said with a growl. "I shouldn't do this." He moved his hands to her small bottom and lifted her into the vee of his hips, into the throbbing part of him that sought what she was offering.

"Oh, Lord," he whispered to himself as he felt the rising tide of desire rack his body. If Caity was ever going to cry, he wished she'd do it now. He didn't think he could pull back. They'd gone too far.

But it was Caitlan who put her hands between

them and rested them on his chest, pushing him away. "Please, John, don't. We can't."

"Don't?"

"I think you know that I won't stop you, but this isn't smart. I'm very much afraid of you."

"No. Never be afraid of me," he said in a desperate tone. "Go to bed, Caitlan. I'll lock up."

She forced herself to slide past him, then she stopped, turned back, and lifted herself to her toes. She brushed his lips lightly with her own. "Thank you, John. The evening was nice."

"Yes it was. Good night, Caitlan. Sleep well."

There was a long silence while Caitlan tried to sort out the contradictory feelings she was experiencing. She could never be devious. If she said anything at all, she'd tell him how much she was beginning to like him. Instead she walked through the living room into her bedroom. She'd play Scarlett O'Hara. She didn't even want to try and analyze the feelings he set off in her. She'd worry about it tomorrow.

"Good night, cowboy."

Four

Caitlan carefully shut the bedroom door. The sound of the ocean was lost behind new locks and closed doors, and some of her tranquility was gone with it. She paced around the room for a moment before admitting that it wasn't the locks that bothered her. It was John Garmon's presence in her loft.

She'd tried not to think about her relationship with John. They were two ships passing in the night, she'd told herself. He'd only be there a short time and then he'd be gone. So there was no reason to dwell on what had happened, no reason to identify and understand his intentions. Of course she couldn't keep the Blazer, it was too much like being bought off. However, the television and Caity's furniture were different. She'd keep them.

How was she going to explain to the owners about the new locks on the beach cottage? she wondered. More important, how was she going to forget the wonderful feeling of having a man around?

Caity made a little sound and moved in her new bed. Caitlan was beside her instantly. She hadn't expected to feel such overwhelming emotion for the child. For the nine months she'd carried her she hadn't allowed herself to think of the baby as hers. She'd focused on the fact that it was Ann's and Jeffrey's baby. And then they were gone, and suddenly she was a mother when she'd been conditioned not to think of herself in the role. She hadn't admitted in the beginning how frightened she was. Even lately when she held the child, she feared that everything was only temporary. Her heart pained her as she acknowledged her true feelings for the first time. She'd planned to show her love by giving Ann and Jeffrey a baby, and the reverse had happened. The gift had been from them to her. Caitlan smoothed the sheet and gave the baby a kiss on her forehead.

For a long time she stood by the bed in the darkness. Her life had changed completely. Change was something she'd never looked on as a problem. Change represented hope. Now change had become the enemy. It had brought John Garmon into her life, and once he'd made his mark, change would take him away. And Caitlan knew that her life would never be the same again.

Defiantly, Caitlan turned off the air conditioner and opened her bedroom window. She stood listening to the whispery slapping of the waves against the sand. Without knowing it she'd been humming while she stood. It took her a moment to realize that the song was the country-music tune they'd heard in the restaurant.

It didn't take her nearly as long to recognize the

familiar rumbling in the pit of her stomach. She thought she'd put all her queasiness behind her after Caity's birth. She should have known better. The emotional excitement of John's presence, followed by shrimp, iced tea, and dancing was about to extort its price. Swallowing hard she dashed toward her bathroom. By the time she'd lost her dinner she was so drained that she could hardly stand. By the time she realized that someone was knocking on her bedroom door, John was inside, lifting her in his arms and carrying her to her bed.

"Who is your doctor?" he demanded gruffly.

"Dr. Eubanks, why?"

"I'm calling him—now!"

John pulled back the cover and laid her on the bed, pushing her hair back from her face anxiously.

"I'm all right, John. I had a little too much excitement and food for one day. I'll be fine, really."

He left her side and began rummaging in her bathroom. She could hear water running and then he was sitting on the bed beside her, wiping her face and neck.

He rinsed the facecloth and gently wiped her face again, trying desperately to still the raging emotion he'd felt when he'd burst through the door and had seen her swaying in the doorway. He'd been so scared. She was pale and her breathing was shallow. She wasn't all right—not yet. He slid his arm behind her and lifted her so that he could draw the straps of her sundress down from her shoulders.

"What are you doing?" She raised up in alarm, groaned, and slumped back to the pillows as her stomach turned over in protest.

"Undressing you. Is this your nightgown? I found

it hanging on the back of the bathroom door under 'our' robe."

"Yes, but I'll do it. Please. I don't need your help, John. You make me . . . uncomfortable. I can look after myself. I just need to lie still for a while. It will pass."

"All right," he agreed reluctantly, continuing to hold her for another moment, "but in the morning we're going to have a little talk with your doctor. I want to hear from him myself that you're fine."

"No!"

Her voice was steady and indomitable. Gathering all her strength, she sat up and glared at him in the light from the open doorway behind him. "I appreciate your concern as a human being, but I'm not a Garmon, and you can't come charging in here giving me orders. This has been a nice day, but it's over. You are not taking me to the doctor. In fact, I really wish you'd get out of here and take that Jeep with you."

"Sorry, babe. I can't do that. Jeffrey left you to me, whether you like it or not. I have to see this through."

"Go away," she said, closing her eyes in desperation. "I don't want the farm and I don't want to run a chocolate factory." She had to get him out of her house—and her life.

"You're not thinking clearly now, Caitlan. You were right to refuse to sell the stock before. We'll talk about it tomorrow."

"No, we won't," Caitlan said with finality. "I won't sell you the stock, but I'll sign any power of attorney forms you want. Just get them ready. I'm very tired, John. And all fun and games aside, you're not my brother."

"This isn't fun and games," he said just as seriously, "and I damn well don't want to be your brother, Caitlan."

John Garmon climbed down the ladder, rubbed his eyes wearily, and took in the quiet, empty feel of the cottage. Caitlan's bedroom door was open and her bed was made. From the deck he looked up and down the beach as far as he could see. She wasn't there. The car was there. The Blazer was there. The powerful new Harley-Davidson he'd bought had been delivered sometime that morning. But Caitlan and the baby were gone.

With growing disbelief he turned back to the kitchen. On the counter were the forms from his attaché case, the forms he'd brought for Caitlan to sign, turning over the control of the stock to him and relinquishing the ownership of the farm. An attached note simply said:

I'm going to visit some friends for a few days. Stay as long as you like and lock up when you leave. Thank you for coming.

"Damn!" John picked up the forms and slapped them against his thigh. He could have put his hands around Caitlan Downey's neck and strangled her. What did she think she was doing, running out on him? Did she actually believe that he'd go meekly back to Savannah after what had happened between them? Well, she had another think coming. He'd said that he was going to make sure she was really all right, and he was going to do just that. He wasn't leaving her until he was satisfied.

John ran his fingers through his hair, shoved his

feet into his running shoes, picked up the keys to the motorcycle from the counter, and locked the cottage door carefully behind him. He didn't try to analyze his anger, he just let it carry him. Straddling the bike, he brought its motor violently to life.

Roaring down the beach highway, he carried on an argument with himself. He ought to do what she said and head back to Savannah. He had work to do. But he couldn't leave Caitlan to raise Jeffrey's child alone. She needed help, the child needed a father—and they needed to do some serious talking. He turned toward the Carnival Strip and drove slowly down the street until he spotted McGraw's Books, a store he knew Caitlan frequented.

The store was housed in the front part of a private residence. The owner nodded as John entered the store, then went back to the newspaper he was reading.

"Have you seen Caitlan?" John said with more force than he'd intended.

"Yep," the man answered without further comment.

"Where is she?"

"Away."

"Away, where?"

"Just away."

"Now see here," John began, and took a threatening step toward Jeb McGraw.

"Nope, you see here." Jeb stood up, towering above John Garmon and outweighing him by more than fifty pounds. "Caitlan is a special lady. She has lots of friends along the Strip and at the moment, you aren't one of them. You'd best just take yourself back to Savannah before I have you arrested for trespassing."

"Trespassing! How the hell can you have me arrested for trespassing in a retail store?"

"We don't open till noon, Mr. Garmon. Until then, this is my house."

"Wait," John said. "I didn't mean to come on so strong. I'm worried about her. She was pretty sick last night. She's not strong, you know."

"We know, and we'll take care of her, Garmon. Go back home." He paused and added more gently, "she'll keep in touch with you, don't worry."

"I'll bet," John said under his breath as he turned and headed toward his bike. He'd played this scene before back in Pretty Springs when he'd searched for Caitlan the first time. He'd been threatened with jail then too. But this time there was no nursing home orderly named Harold to steer him in the right direction. Fine, he decided, Ms. Greta Garbo Downey wanted to be left alone, he'd leave her alone! He didn't need the aggravation anyway.

The downtown area of the amusement strip was about two blocks long and consisted of a drugstore, a small grocery store, a dentist's and a doctor's office. John hit the brakes in front of the doctor's office, stopped the bike, and walked inside.

The white-haired, elderly receptionist looked up, caught sight of John, and shook her head. "Good morning, what can I do for you, young man?"

"My name is Garmon," John began hesitantly, wondering if he'd run into another of Caitlan's protectors. "I'm wondering if Caitlan is—?"

"Garmon?" the receptionist interrupted with a shake of her head. "So you're Jeffrey Garmon? Well, it's about time you stopped shilly-shallying around and got down here. Shame on you, making Caitlan go through all that by herself, and her having such a hard time of it."

"What do you mean? Is she all right?"

"Why, of course she is. She and that darling baby have already been in for her checkup this morning."

He was tired of being the bad guy. He'd never played a heavy in his life, and this charade had gone far enough. He'd just have a talk with the doctor and get a few facts before he confronted Caitlan.

"Where is the good doctor? I'd like to see him immediately."

"He's gone to Jacksonville to attend a meeting. He won't be back until Monday. What you'd better do is go home and shave, and comb your hair before Caitlan sees you."

John glanced into the mirror on the wall opposite the receptionist desk and shook his head. No wonder Jeb McGraw bristled so when he'd asked about Caitlan. He wasn't sure that even he recognized himself. That's what she'd done to him in three days, turned him into a refugee from Hell's Angels. He smiled at the white-haired woman.

"I'm truly sorry, Nurse Ratched," he said with honey dripping from his voice, and a prayer that she hadn't seen *One Flew Over the Cuckoo's Nest*. "When I woke up, Caitlan was gone, and I was so worried that I didn't even stop to get ready. I don't suppose she said where she was going next, did she? I don't want her to be alone now that I'm here."

"Well . . . I suppose she shouldn't be alone. I think she's gone to water the plants at Miss Essie's house. Essie's visiting her sister in Memphis. If she's not there, she'll be over at the nursing home helping out. You know Caitlan, she's always helping out."

"I know, the dear girl." John broadened his smile. "Where is Miss Essie's house?"

"Go back to the corner and turn left. It's the last house on the road."

John started out the door, stopped, and turned back. "By the way, how'd she manage to get down here?"

"Marty, from the motorcycle dealership, brought her here. And I think she caught a ride out to Essie's with Tony the postman."

Wonderful. Marty had delivered his motorcycle just in time to help Caitlan escape. No question about it, Caitlan was a modern-day Billy the Kid with a network of get-away friends as widespread as some western outlaw. She didn't need the Lone Ranger to rescue her. After what she'd done he should be arresting her as a criminal. She'd stolen his name, turned his psyche inside out, and totally screwed up his thinking processes.

And Jeffrey hadn't helped matters any by leaving that note. He didn't know why he was upset. He hadn't learned anything new. Caitlan Downey had given birth to his brother's child. Hell, he thought, he could understand Jeff's desire for a child. The dumpling had gotten to him too. But where did that leave him? Did Caitlan honestly think he could go off and leave his niece to live such an unstructured existence? Look what it had done to Caitlan and Ann, he told himself.

Caitlan. Try as he might he couldn't really fault her. What a fighter she was, ready to defy him and the Garmons all the way, ready to run away from him when she could have almost anything she wanted, including him. He'd fallen under her spell himself. He'd spent most of the night listening for her, worrying about her, until he was satisfied that she was sleeping easily. What in hell was he going to do now?

He reached Essie's house and saw Caitlan, Caity strapped in the pouch on her back, walking on the beach. Shoulders bent, eyes on the ground, she looked like she'd just been told that her sea captain's ship had gone down and that she was totally alone.

John killed the engine and set the bike on its stand. Halfway down the beach he slowed his run to a walk and his rage to an honest admission of frustrated relief. She looked so alone, so lovely.

"Caitlan?"

"John. How did you find us?"

"More of your walking on water. It gave you away. I went to your doctor's office, and the nurse told me you'd be here."

They were standing inches apart. Her lower lip was stiff and proud, daring him to challenge her. But behind the bravado he felt something more, something that made him want to take her in his arms and tell her everything would be all right. She seemed so innocent, so vulnerable. Damn! She was doing it to him again. Without a word she'd turned his bones into jelly.

"Let's go home, Caitlan. We have to talk."

He'd been to her doctor's office, she realized. He couldn't have found out everything, could he? Part of her trembled at what that knowledge could mean and part of her wanted him to know. Sooner or later he was bound to find out, and she was torn between the vow of secrecy she'd sworn to and her need to be honest with him. She wished she'd never promised Ann and Jeffrey to protect their secret. They hadn't known what it would mean. "You aren't going to leave, are you, John?"

"I can't—not yet."

He took her hand and pulled her up the sandy incline to the road where he'd left his motorcycle. "Do you think you can hang on to my back?"

Caitlan simply nodded and took the helmet he handed her and fastened it beneath her chin. She was too tired and miserable to argue.

The only awkward moment came when Caitlan slid onto the seat behind John. All peace of mind flew straight out into the blue summer sky when she folded her arms around John Garmon and felt the startled contractions of the muscles beneath her grasp.

Caitlan remembered the last time she'd put her arms around him and she knew that letting John Garmon stay on in her little beach cottage was a mistake. Somehow she had to convince him to take his paperwork and go, before he found out more than he ought to know, before he got too close to the truth.

"John, are you sure we won't get into trouble for having a baby ride on the motorcycle?"

"I'm with you now, the woman who can do no wrong. The police will probably give us a personal escort."

His controlled voice didn't sound like that of a carefree biker. In fact, everything about the man said that he was tense, even angry—very angry. The engine roared to life and talking was suddenly impossible as he moved the powerful machine back onto the highway and away from the Strip.

"It feels as if we're flying through space," Caitlan yelled, hearing her words jerked away on the wind. "This is wonderful."

The trip back to the cottage was made carefully. She could tell by the stiffness of John's body that she'd better be prepared to have her world come crashing down as soon as he began their talk. But for now the warmth of the sun beading her scalp with perspiration and her body with electric tingles seemed not at all out of place in their flight from reality.

The beach cottage came into view much too quickly and Caitlan's fantasy died a cold death as John slid off the bike, took her by the hand, and dragged her up the steps and into the cottage.

"Now. Put the baby down for a nap and come sit here on the couch. I want answers and I want them now."

There was to be no arguing with the man standing before her. His hair was windblown. He hadn't shaved. His face was covered with a gold-brown stubble of beard.

"What's wrong, John?"

"I was in your doctor's office this morning, after you left."

"Why?"

"I was worried about you, dammit. You nearly passed out on me last night, and this morning you were gone—visiting friends?" His voice was incredulous. "What kind of game are you playing, babe?"

"No game, John. I'm just carrying on with my life. I don't ask you to approve of it."

"Well, I don't," he said, then wished he could take back the words. He didn't want to argue with Caitlan. He wanted her to have faith in him. He didn't know what he was going to do yet, but his mixed emotions about her were playing havoc with his plans. "I was asked to come here and look after you and the baby, Caitlan, and that's what I'm bound to do. Please trust me."

And she was bound to silence, she wanted to say, no matter what she might want to do. "I didn't ask you to come here, John. I appreciate what you're trying to do, but I have to make my own decisions—about myself and Caity. Maybe someday things will be different. Go home, John."

"Sure, and you'll send us a snapshot on the baby's birthday and a card at Christmas. No way." There had been a finality in her voice that forced him to lose all control. "No! Let's be honest, Caitlan. You need my help. You can't look after Caity and yourself. Babies need stability. You're coming to Savannah where I can supervise her upbringing."

"I'm what?" Caitlan blanched. "Who gave you the right to give me orders?" She wouldn't give in to the urge to slap his face and throw him out of her cottage. She couldn't afford to give in to anger. She might make a mistake. And no matter how she might feel, she had no choice but to be calm and unruffled. She had a natural claim on Caity and she intended to keep her.

Well, he'd blown it now, he thought. He might as well say it all. "Who gave me the right? First Jeffrey, with his request that I look after you. Then you, when you let your little gang believe that I'm Caity's father. What'd you tell them, anyway? That I was some kind of villain?"

This much of the truth she owed him. "I didn't know what might happen. If I . . . well, if things didn't go right, you'd have to know. I just told Jeb and Danni that Caity's father could be reached at the Garmon Chocolate Company. I wanted to protect Caity, but I was afraid they might try to contact you, so I told them her father was a married man."

"You what?"

"Well, he was. He was married to my sister. My explanation seemed . . . simpler at the time."

"Fine. Then I doubt seriously that any court in the world would refuse to allow a father to oversee his child's future. Oh, Caitlan, no matter what you might think, that makes me responsible."

She didn't answer.

"The nurse thought I was Jeffrey," he went on quietly. "She told me what a terrible person I was to let you go through this alone. Why didn't you ask for our help? Why, Caitlan?" he questioned.

"Does it matter?" Her voice was so low that he could barely hear it. She couldn't stand seeing the hurt in his eyes. She wanted to tell him the truth. She hurt with the pain of her deceit.

His mouth was stern as he contemplated the unspoken answer to his question.

He was hurting. She was hurting, too, but she couldn't tell him the truth. "Stop this. It only makes it worse. I'm me and you're you, and we live in very different spaces," she said softly. "And you have no right to question me. The past is done and we can't change it. You don't belong here, and I'd really like it if you'd leave."

"Oh, sure, I'm going to leave, Ms. Downey. I'm going home and I'll have to tell my mother, guess what, you have a grandchild. Jeffrey is the father. Ann couldn't have a child so her sister did it for her. But she doesn't want to share the child so she'll raise her alone. She'll really love you for that, Caitlan."

Caitlan stared at him. He should have been dark and menacing, wearing a black hat and a patch over one eye. But he wasn't dark and menacing. He was the golden-haired cowboy who'd charged in to rescue the fair young maiden. The young maiden, however, turned out to be a stubborn, determined woman who wanted to make her own decisions. It wasn't John's fault, and she couldn't tell him the truth.

Only that morning, while she was walking with Caity on the beach did she begin to understand that what she was feeling for John Garmon was the kind of caring she'd watched develop between Ann and Jeffrey. She had to stop it before it got out of hand. The hero always ended up with the schoolmarm, not the outcast. The small world of Savannah, Georgia society would never accept Caitlan Downey in their inner circle.

With sadness she continued softly. "The baby is mine, John. Mine. Leave us alone. I don't expect anything from you or your mother. The stock is mine too. Jeffrey left it to me, and I'll not dishonor his wishes. But I don't want anything else. You may vote my shares. I think it would be better if we don't see each other again."

She thought all he was interested in was the stock, he realized. She sat there like some kind of old-world Madonna, proud and aloof. She wasn't going to explain or demand anything. She intended to relinquish her hold on the family. She was tough, this dark-eyed, winsome creature—tough like a fragile, delicate sapling growing from the side of a sheer rocky cliff. It would be buffeted by any strong wind and it couldn't be broken.

John Garmon mentally shook himself. He must be losing his grip on reality. He ought to jerk her up and shake some sense into her. He ought to . . .

She stood up and he grabbed her by her shoulders. Her face was only inches from his, and all he wanted to do was kiss her. With a groan, he shoved her away and tore past her out of the cabin. Damn, he thought. He'd wanted to make it up to Jeffrey by caring for Caitlan and the child, and all he felt was a deep, boiling anger—anger that the child she'd borne had belonged to his brother when he wished it had been his instead.

Fine, she wanted him to leave. That's what he'd do. But first he'd finish what he'd started. He arranged to have the house stocked with more groceries than Caitlan would use in a year. He deposited a large sum of money in a special checking account for Caitlan Downey, and he hired a very prissy nanny named Mrs. French who had excellent references and needed temporary work to earn enough money to be able to return to her daughter's house in New Jersey. He drove away that evening while Caitlan was at work.

Mrs. French arrived the next morning to begin caring for Caity. That afternoon Caitlan found out Mrs. French was really Mrs. Peterson and that her granddaughter's health had forced both the girl's mother and the grandmother to find work to support themselves. The next morning Caitlan with-

drew the last of her own funds from her own bank
account and gave the money and the Blazer to the
woman and sent her on her way to New Jersey.

Caitlan was alone again. Life was back to normal,
but the cottage was different. Caitlan was different.
She was forced to admit that the difference had to
do with John. She found being alone, for the first
time in her twenty-eight years, lonely.

John's second stop in Pretty Springs was as frustrating and uninformative as it had been the first
time. Yes, Caitlan Downey had worked at the Pretty
Springs Nursing Home. She'd been first cousin to a
saint and twice as mysterious. She had no personal
life, no *close* friends, no warts or dishonorable char-
acteristics. She had no past and no future. In short
she truly walked on water, and from the Chief of
Police to the same rotund orderly who'd given him
his original information on Caitlan's destination,
the citizens of the small town closed ranks and threatened him with incarceration or worse—if he did
anything to hurt this paragon of virtue. After three
days he gave up and flew back to Savannah, no
wiser but more miserable than he'd been when he'd
left Florida.

His new plan was to fling himself back into his
work and find a woman who appreciated him. The
first week he tried. The second week he wished that
he'd never gone to Florida to find Caitlan Downey.
He snapped at his mother, skipped the weekly planning meeting at the candy factory, and wrecked his
favorite motorcycle. By the end of the third week he
knew that he had to go back. He had to tell Caitlan

that he'd bought the beach cottage. She probably wasn't eating properly, and the chances were that she still was working two shifts so that some poor soul could attend a funeral, or a wedding, or go on a retreat to some Tibetan monastery with a guru who practiced free love and made moonshine on the side.

Jeffrey had left the farm and the stock to Caitlan. He intended her to be cared for, and John didn't have the right to go against his brother's wishes. Caitlan Downey's welfare was his concern, and he was fooling around in Savannah while she was alone with Caity on a Florida beach. What kind of respect was he showing Jeffrey?

"I'm going back to Florida, Mother," he said at breakfast one morning.

"I thought you might," Mrs. Garmon said. "Something back there isn't settled yet, am I correct?"

"Yes. I may stay for a while, Mother. Can you manage here without me?"

She gave him a keen, knowing look. "Of course, John. I don't understand the problem with the woman, but I've come to believe that Jeffrey had his reasons for doing what he did, and I'm sure you'll do what's best for the family and the company. I won't ask any questions, and I'll support your decisions, whatever they are."

John knew his mother was waiting for an explanation, but she hadn't pressed him. At least she'd learned to stand back and let him work out his own solutions. She hadn't done that with Jeffrey and she'd pushed him away. Her mistake had been painful, and whatever Mettie Garmon was, she wasn't stupid. Trying to change her sons was a mistake she wouldn't commit again, John realized.

"How long will you be away?"

"I'm not sure." Hell, he didn't even know what he expected to accomplish. He only knew that he couldn't concentrate on his work or fit back into the life-style he'd always enjoyed. Every time he closed his eyes she was with him, her dark eyes beseeching him with veiled passion and unacknowledged desire. He found himself listening for the baby, missing her curl the tiny rosebud of a mouth into a smile. He was drawn to them, and he couldn't seem to forget. He had to go back.

"Shall I make a plane reservation for you?"

"No, I'll make my own."

He didn't.

He chartered a private plane, hired a rental car at the Pensacola airport, and drove as though he were the outlaw with the posse on his trail—but he was too late. The Blazer was gone. The cottage was empty. All signs of life were gone from the little beach house. Caity's white crib with the pink and blue bears was made up and waiting, but Caitlan Downey and her child were gone.

If she was at work and he burst in, the police probably would arrest him. If he went looking for her in town, Jeb McGraw probably would break him in half and stomp on his bones. Wherever she was, she wouldn't be gone long. Sooner or later one of her gang would wander in. He'd wait. When she came back, they'd talk. He wouldn't make accusations or ask questions. He wouldn't insist that she make any changes in her life-style. He'd wait for her to make the first move. He'd just be there—for her.

John sat on the front steps and felt his eyes swim with moisture. Suppose she wouldn't allow him to stay? He'd rushed into her life ready to demand that she stay out of the Garmon family and she'd agreed without a fuss. Now he found that he couldn't walk away. Whatever game he'd been playing was just that—a game. He wasn't Gene Autry, or the Lone Ranger, or Luke Skywalker. He wasn't even a good "bad guy."

He was simply John Garmon—stuffed shirt, member of the board, card-carrying, certified bully, and he wanted very much to change his image. He grinned. Being a "kinky" jerk had been a lot more fun. Inside the cabin he changed into a pair of black shorts and a black Hawaiian print shirt. As he walked morosely around, he tried desperately to remember the tune to Randy Travis's she-done-me-wrong song, but he couldn't.

The morning passed and John Garmon sat, waiting for the woman who got away.

Five

A rough sound broke through John's misery like a pebble dropped into a silent pool. He lifted his head as Tony the postman started down the path to the cottage.

"Hey, man," Tony called out in disgust, "where've you been? Caitlan and the baby both end up in the hospital and you aren't even here."

"Hospital?" John came swiftly to his feet. "When?"

"Three days ago."

By the time Tony answered the question, John was halfway to his car. For the first time since he began his search for Caitlan Downey, he gave her law-and-order friends a legitimate reason to have him arrested. He'd always been reckless on his bike, but in an automobile John Garmon never exceeded the speed limit. This time he ran two red lights and a stop sign. When the hospital came into view, he pulled right up to the door, came to a screeching stop, killed the engine, and dashed up the steps.

"Caitlan, Caitlan Downey! Where is she?" he demanded of the startled receptionist at the visitors desk.

"Second floor. The elevator is on your right. She's in room . . ." John left the receptionist talking to thin air. He was already at the top of the steps. He burst into the hallway.

"Just a minute, sir!" one of the nurses called out. "This is the maternity ward. You aren't allowed in here now, unless you're a father. It's feeding time."

"Caitlan Downey. Where is she?" John watched the quick frown leave the nurse's face as she got a good look at the panic spread across his own.

"Other end of the hall, first door on the left. But you'll have to check in at the nursing station, Mr.—?"

"Garmon, my name is Garmon."

"But—"

The nursing station came into view. "Caitlan Downey. Where is she?" he asked again.

"Visiting hours don't begin for an hour," the nurse protested, taking in the blond giant of a man wearing the garish shirt and no shoes. "Are you a relative?"

"Yes! I'm her . . . a . . . the father of her child. Please?" he added softly.

"You'll have to wear a mask and gown."

"I'll take off my clothes and go nude. Just get me to her!"

The nurse smothered a smile. "That'd liven up this place."

In a few minutes he was standing in the doorway of Caitlan's room. She was holding the child. John caught his breath. With the soft light falling across her dark hair, and with her wide eyes all soft and dreamy, Caitlan Downey was the loveliest thing John had ever seen. He stopped inside the door and waited, unwilling to interrupt the moment. Murmuring loving little sounds, Caitlan was feeding the child he'd nicknamed 'dumpling.'

"Caitlan?"

"Oh!" She looked up and recognized John. "You do have style, John Garmon." Her eyes glowed as she smiled at him. "And you definitely have aristocratic knees."

He looked down at his bare legs exposed by the blue paper robe they'd insisted he wear and smiled beneath the paper mask across his mouth. "Kinky, aristocratic knees," he corrected.

"You came back. How did you know we needed you?"

"I didn't, Tony told me." He crossed the room, surprised at how calmly she accepted his presence, "I never should have left you. Are you okay?"

"Oh, yes." She nodded, pulling the sheet modestly across her body.

"Why are you on the maternity floor?" He lifted an eyebrow.

Caitlan shifted the child and laid a kiss on her cheek. "Since I'm on the staff here, they bent the rules a little and moved me to the same floor as the nursery so that I could be near Caity."

John walked across the room and stood by the bed looking down at the mother and child. Caity followed the sound of his voice and rewarded him with a happy smile. "Hi, dumpling, are you glad to see me?"

"She's going to be fine, John. She's a very special little girl."

"Oh, yes," he answered softly, knowing that it wasn't the child he was referring to. Be careful, John, he cautioned himself. You're in danger of being caught up in the universal beauty of motherhood.

He reached down and caught Caity's tiny hand in his big long fingers. "What happened, Caitlan?"

"We both had some kind of weird virus. I apparently picked it up at the hospital and gave it to Caity. We were both pretty sick," she admitted gravely, "but we're over it now."

"And Mrs. French?"

"Mrs. French?" Caitlan echoed hesitantly.

"Yes, Mrs. French, the nanny I hired before I left. Where would she be?"

Caitlan winced. "I dismissed her."

"You what?" John cried out, then dropped his voice. "Why did you dismiss the woman? Her references were very good and you needed help."

"Because she was a stiff-necked tyrant," Caitlan said belligerently. "No, she wasn't. She was probably a very nice person, but she had her own ideas and I had mine. And you didn't ask me what I thought and . . . well . . . I want to raise my child—my own way."

"And the Blazer?"

Misery lined Caitlan's face and she leaned her head back and closed her eyes for a second. He might as well hear it all. She'd hoped that the Blazer would be back before she had to account for it, but that wasn't to be. "I loaned it to Mrs. French to drive to New Jersey. She has a daughter who lives outside of town and a grandchild who has to go into the hospital for six weeks of special therapy. They needed transportation."

"So you just gave her a ten-thousand-dollar vehicle because she needed it?"

"No, I loaned it to her. She's going to return the Blazer and pay me ba . . ." The words began in a rush and trailed off when she realized that she'd told him the very thing she didn't mean to.

"How much money did you give her? No, never mind, I don't want to know. Why didn't you call me and let me handle it?"

"I wanted to," she admitted, "but I knew you'd probably buy her a bus ticket and . . . well, I know it was dumb. But after I found out why she needed the money, I felt responsible. I'm sorry if you're upset, John, but I wouldn't have felt right keeping her here when her own family needed her, would I?"

"No, I guess not. But you could have called me when you got sick."

"If I had you'd have put the staff of Johns Hopkins University on a jet and sent them down, or something equally as dumb."

"Probably," he admitted with a smile. "We're both pretty foolish, you know. You take on the whole world. I'm more selective. I'm only concerned with one woman and one wee babe." Caitlan was pale but beautiful. Her skin seemed even more translucent and finely drawn across her face. "You don't seem surprised to see me."

"I'm not. I knew you'd come."

"Does that distress you?"

"Yes, I think it does, and I think it distresses you, too, John, because you don't understand it. If it makes you feel any better, neither do I."

He felt as if she could get inside his mind and read the confusion he was feeling. He wanted to yell at her, to demand honest explanations, to take her in his arms and hold her. "I'm sorry I left."

"I'm sorry you came back. It will just complicate things, you know."

"I know."

Caity held tightly to his finger. He felt the cool cotton of Caitlan's nightgown and her heart beating rapidly beneath his hand. Loosening his finger from Caity's grasp, he slid his hand slowly up Caitlan's neck, pushing her dark hair behind one ear and following the curve of her cheekbone to her lips.

Caitlan lay still, staring at him with open eyes, barely breathing as his fingers lightly skimmed her face. She'd known he'd return, even wished for him. At one point when she'd been sickest, she'd given the doctor his name to be notified if . . . Then she'd begun to get better.

"This is the first time I've nursed her since I got sick," Caitlan said shyly. "They were concerned that my milk would make her worse. Now I'm afraid my milk is drying up."

Caitlan adjusted her gown self-consciously. The child flung back one tiny hand and opened her eyes again, eyes that seemed to reach out and touch John with their special dreamlike quality.

"I'm sorry," John said simply. He knew that not being able to nurse the baby must bother Caitlan, and he felt her despair. He liked watching her nurse Caity. "There must be a formula the doctor can prescribe for her. We'll get whatever she needs."

"I know, but it makes me feel less important, inadequate, and I've never felt that way before."

Her voice broke and she turned her head away.

"Caitlan, darling, you're very important." John continued to stroke her face and hair. "It isn't only food for the body that you give, it's love."

Caitlan lifted her gaze to the man she'd feared, and in that moment, when her gaze met his, she knew. It wasn't fear that she felt for John Garmon. It was something much stronger. His thick tawny hair had grown longer. For the three weeks he'd been away he'd let it grow until it fell in layered waves to his collar and curled around his ears. He was a golden man, a true warrior, and she knew that she was falling in love with him.

When he'd held her at the funeral, she knew he was special. Now that she was too tired and weak to fight her feelings, she was forced to acknowledge what she'd suspected all along. She needed him and his stubborn strength. From the time Ann and Jeffrey had married and taken her into their circle of love, she'd been blessed. Her life had rushed along at a wonderfully happy pace. She'd existed, she'd related to everyone around her, but never in her life had she lived for herself. Then John had come along and she couldn't fight him anymore.

When he ripped off his hospital mask, she protested, "Suppose you catch something?"

"I don't care," he whispered.

As he lowered his head she lay very still, waiting for the touch of his lips on hers. She felt her lips part beneath his, accepting him with the quiet promise of her love. Suddenly she was warm. Her blood began to sing in her veins, and she felt more alive than she'd felt since Caity was born.

The bed gave under the pressure of his body as he sat down and gathered her and Caity into his arms. His second kiss was short and gentle. It was the embrace that he prolonged. He held them both, gently touching her face and shoulder and the silky cap of hair on Caity's head. It seemed natural and good to feel his arms around her. She leaned against him, absorbing him as though his touch were a transfusion of strength.

"Mr. Garmon, it's time for you to leave. Ms. Downey is still very weak. You can come back this evening."

John heard the words the nurse was speaking. He heard and obeyed her command in an hypnotic trance. More shaken than he realized, John allowed himself to be led down the hall to a visitors waiting area. He sank into an overstuffed chair and blinked. He was having a hard time assimilating the emotions whirling around inside his head.

Caitlan Downey, the mother of his brother's child, had driven him crazy for these last few weeks. And now that he'd seen her again he was more confused than ever. The only thing he knew for sure was that he wanted to make Caitlan and the child his own.

"Mr. Garmon?"

"Yes?"

The man in the doorway was wearing green surgical garb and a stern expression on his face. Around his neck hung a mask, and his shoes were covered with matching green coverings.

"I'm Walt Eubanks, Caitlan's doctor. I'm glad you're here. She had a pretty rough time of it. We had to perform an emergency c-section when the baby came, and she just hasn't gotten her strength back. Then she came down with this damn fool virus. All things considered, having a healthy child wasn't an easy task for Caitlan. She could never have managed a multiple birth."

"Multiple birth? What do you mean?"

"Well, I'm certain you know how many times in vitro fertilization results in multiple births. Only because the initial egg to be fertilized was her own sister's, did they take the chance on single implantation. Even then we couldn't be certain that there was only one child until she delivered."

"One egg?" John murmured woodenly.

"Caitlan was much too small to carry several babies and she might not have survived the trauma," the doctor went on. "Then to be hit with a virus so soon afterward, well, I can tell you I was worried for a couple of days. But we're certain that there was no connection between this illness and the method of conception."

"In vitro . . . in vitro fertilization?" John's mind was suddenly struck with the reality of the man's words. In vitro fertilization—her *sister's* egg, fertilized by his brother, being implanted in Caitlan's body. John came to his feet, his anguish turning into a faint glimmer of understanding.

"I can't say that I'm thrilled with the way you two have handled any of this," the doctor went on. "She should never have come here that late in her pregnancy. She should have stayed in touch with the doctor who did the tests and performed the fertilization."

"Uh, yes. You're right," John agreed seriously. He tried to keep a smile from his face. The doctor would think he'd lost his mind, but he couldn't suppress his relief at knowing that he had as much claim to Caity as Caitlan did.

"I trust that your wife has taken the proper hormone therapy to produce milk so that she can nurse the child as you'd planned? I don't think Caitlan will be able to do it after this little bout of infection."

"No! I mean . . . you don't understand. Jeffrey, my brother, is the child's father. Jeffrey and his wife Ann were killed in a boating accident. I'm Jeffrey's brother, John Garmon, and I didn't know about any of these details until now."

The doctor blanched. His face went white with shock. "Hell! You mean you're not Jeffrey Garmon, the father of the baby? You haven't come to claim the child as agreed? Damn! Caitlan swore me to secrecy."

"I'm claiming the baby, yes. I'm the only family Caitlan has. Please, don't tell her that I know. If Caitlan doesn't have enough milk, we can work out something else, can't we?"

"Yes, certainly. I'll leave instructions with the staff. Truthfully, it's good that you're here, though I don't know what Caitlan will say when she finds out. She's going to need nursing care for several days."

"Fine. I'll engage a nurse and take her home. Don't worry, Dr. Eubanks. Everything will be fine. I promise you."

"All right," he agreed reluctantly, anxious now to be away from the problem. "If you're sure. I'll make the arrangements for a nurse. You may plan to transfer them tomorrow."

John couldn't resist peeking into Caitlan's room before he left. She was sleeping. Her hair formed a fine mist of black on the pillow, and the light blanket hugged her body, emphasizing how small and fragile she was. He stood over her bed for a long time, fighting the urge to touch her. In vitro fertilization. Caitlan Downey was one very special lady. She probably *could* walk on water, if she set her mind to it.

"Mr. Garmon, you have enough supplies here to outfit the nursery at the Children's Hospital." Sarah Flanagan surveyed the crowded cottage and shook her head. "It will be months before that child needs all these toys."

"I know," John agreed with a boyish grin, "but I couldn't resist. How do you like her crib?" He stood back admiring his earlier selection unashamedly. The antique crib had a new lacey spread, covered with assorted stuffed bears and a large furry unicorn with a gold satin horn.

"It's beautiful, though I'm not certain that she'll have room to sleep. Hadn't you better go and get her?"

"Yes, I'll get the car."

John stepped outside the door straight into a procession of automobiles. In the first vehicle, a limousine, was Caitlan, sitting beside Jeb McGraw with Caity in her arms. Behind the limo was Tony in the mail truck, then Danni in her orange Honda. Laughing, they all piled out of the convoy and followed Caitlan down the walk and onto the deck.

"What are all of you doing here?" John asked ungraciously.

"Oh, it's the chocolate king," Danni said with exaggerated lust. "Nice of you to drop in again, you extra sweet morsel of delight."

"Caitlan said you'd be here," Jeb McGraw said. "Why?"

"I'm the father's bro . . . I'm the father," he declared loudly as he stood in the door and glowered at the group.

"The married father?" Jeb took a step toward John.

"No, wait, Jeb." Caitlan moved to John's side and slid her arm around his waist. "John isn't married. He never was. I only told you all that to keep you from calling him. I appreciate your helping me home, but I'd like you to go now."

"Are you sure you don't want us to throw the jerk out?" one of the women in the back yelled out.

"No. That won't be necessary," Caitlan said with quiet dignity. "John lives here with me. Thank you all for your support, but I think I'd like you to go. I am a little tired."

Immediately everyone in the procession turned and began to leave, offering assistance, transportation, and anything else Caitlan might need. She kissed each one of them and whispered something private to each of them before turning back wearily to John.

Caitlan smiled wanly for a moment. "I think you'd better take Caity," she whispered as she held out the baby to the open-mouthed nurse who'd appeared in the doorway. "John?" She began to slump forward into his arms.

John carried Caitlan into the house and laid her on the bed. "Just a typical Downey gang jailbreak, huh?" John knew he was being unreasonably irritable but the look on Caitlan's face when she turned to him had scared him silly. Besides, he admitted, he'd wanted to be the one to bring Caitlan and the child home. He removed Caitlan's shoes and covered her legs with the spread. She breathed shallowly for a few minutes, then opened her eyes and glanced around.

"Oh, John, I'm glad I'm home. Thank you for hiring the nurse, but I wish you hadn't bought all these new things. I'll just have to move them when I leave here."

"No you won't, I . . ." He remembered her pride, her claim that she'd care for herself, and swallowed the words he'd been about to say. He'd tell her later that he'd bought the cottage for her. Knowing what he knew about her, if he told her, she was likely to pack up and move into a tent on the beach. "Well, I couldn't have our baby sleep in a drawer, now could I? What would people think about my rescue service?"

Sarah Flanagan, the nurse, placed the baby on her stomach in the crib and covered her with a light blanket. She turned back to John and motioned him out of the room with her head. "I'll take over, Mr. Garmon. You go and find yourself something to do out there. Your wife needs to rest."

Wife? John stared at Caitlan without speaking. She opened her eyes and touched her fingertips to her hair. There was something regal about her movements. She was pale and tired. Still she managed an embarrassed smile. "I know I look like some kind of outlaw on the lam, John, but give me a few days, and I'll challenge you to a quick-draw contest at high noon."

"You don't look awful, Caitlan. You look lovely." He wanted to reach down and put his arms around her again. She needed reassuring. He wanted to tell her that he knew the truth about Caity. He wanted her to tell him the truth. He wanted her to know how wonderful he thought her gesture had been. But it wasn't the right time. She was exhausted. He'd let her rest, and they'd talk later. "Besides, what would a cowboy do without outlaws?"

"Herd cows, I suppose, John. But thank you anyway," she said softly and took his hand. "You're very kind. I just wish . . ."

There was an awkwardness about her uncertainty that hadn't been there before. "I know. You wish I'd go away and leave you alone. But I can't, not yet. Not until you're strong again. Jeffrey and Ann could come back and haunt me."

"Ah, Gene Autry to the rescue," she murmured, her eyelids heavy with exhaustion. "Did you bring your white horse?"

"Not this time, Caitlan. I did a little research while I was back in Savannah. It was Hop Along Cassidy who rode the white horse."

Caitlan giggled. "You really watched old cowboy movies? Miss Mettie must have thought you'd lost your marbles."

"My mother learned the first afternoon to stay out of my way. Besides, I live on the top floor of Garmon House in completely separate quarters."

"My, my, the Garmon House must be awfully big."

"Yes, and awfully quiet. I missed you," he admitted.

"And I missed you too. . . ." Her voice trailed off and he knew that she was falling asleep.

John leaned down and kissed her forehead and her cheek. She was such a stubborn woman, so lovely, so trusting. He didn't understand her decision to have this child for his brother and sister-in-law, but the more he learned about Caitlan Downey, the more he was intrigued. She was no scheming opportunist. She never had been. He'd wait. Sooner or later she'd tell him the truth. In sleep she relaxed the hand she'd been holding and let it fall back across her body. He could feel the swell of her breast, and he jerked his hand away in confusion.

Careful, John Garmon, she's getting to you. There's a whole ocean out there for her to walk on, and you're beginning to believe that she really can do it.

John stood up and caught the smile on Sarah's face. He blushed guiltily and backed away from the bed.

"She's very tired, Mr. Garmon. You'd probably be better off not to share her bed for a day or two. I'll have to be in and out, caring for Caity. Why don't you give her a few weeks, and you'll have your girl back again. Then you'll send me packing. I promise."

"My girl? Share her bed?" he repeated under his breath. Sarah Flanagan hadn't been on the front deck when the exchange over his marital status had taken place. He didn't know what Walt Eubanks had told her, but she obviously thought that he and Caitlan were married. He wasn't sure what he thought about her mistake. He wasn't the child's father, although he knew it was a natural assumption, and he hadn't made any attempt to correct any of their wrong impressions. He wasn't Caitlan's husband, and she wasn't his girl. If he crawled into bed with her she'd probably jump up, find a gun, and shoot him. But, Lordy, he thought, how nice the idea sounded.

He slipped up to the loft and changed into a pair of swimming trunks and a polo shirt. He'd take a quick swim and tackle the mountain of work he'd brought with him from Savannah, he decided. If Caitlan and the baby were going to keep him away from his office, he had better get something done until he figured out how to run a Georgia company from a Florida beach. Actually, it had been years since he'd taken a vacation, so he might as well enjoy himself.

What he ultimately had to do was convince her to move to Savannah. In Savannah his family could give her the support and help she needed with the baby. In Savannah he'd forget the feelings he was experiencing for her. He'd be able to approach the problem from a safer direction.

Two hours later he was shuffling figures on the sales reports in his hand and staring off into the peaceful blue waters of the Gulf. There was something soothing about the scene, and he felt incredibly happy. He felt closer to Jeffrey than he had in years. Behind him in the house he could hear the nurse moving around. Occasionally the baby cried and was hushed just as quickly. He couldn't identify the mood he was in, he just knew that what he felt was something new, a satisfaction that he'd never experienced before. As the sun began to set he laughed lightly. If he had a guitar he might consider serenading his señorita.

Three days later he was learning all about frustration. Caitlan hardly had come out of her room when he was in the cottage. She'd been pleasant enough when he'd poked his head through the door and made some kind of comment, but she hadn't invited him in and he hadn't forced his way. He couldn't concentrate on his paperwork. His telephone calls back to Savannah were less than satisfactory. His mother didn't ask about anything, but he knew that she was as confused as he.

Suddenly Caity began to wail, and John came to his feet in a panic. He'd been sitting in the darkness on the deck. Caitlan had eaten dinner in her room. The nurse had made the couch into a bed just as she did every evening, and the lights in the cottage had been turned off for the night.

The bedroom door opened and closed again in the darkness, and the crying increased in volume. John paced back and forth outside the hateful door, wondering what was happening inside. He strode into the kitchen, opened the refrigerator door and closed it again without seeing what was inside. Above the refrigerator he found a bottle of brandy. He removed the cap and took a long swig of the liquid, then turned and spit it into the sink. After what seemed to be an eternity the door opened again, and Sarah padded back toward the couch with Caity over her shoulder

"What's wrong?" John asked gruffly.

"Nothing abnormal, Mr. Garmon." Her voice was laced with amusement. "Just a little colic from Caity's new formula. She's learning to show her discomfort loudly."

"Oh!" John felt foolish. "May I help?"

"Yes. If you'll hold her a minute, I'll get her medication."

John took Caity, feeling her tiny body contort with spasms of pain. Following the nurse's lead, he walked back and forth, patting her back as he whispered in her ear. Before Sarah Flanagan returned he was rewarded with a huge burp, after which Caity relaxed and quickly went to sleep.

Caitlan, watching from the darkness of the bedroom, scurried to her bed and covered her eyes with her arm, pretending that she was asleep as John entered the room and stood in the darkness.

"Looks as though she prefers the masculine touch," Sarah whispered. "Can't say I blame her. Go to bed, Mr. Garmon. Your wife is nearly back to normal, and any day now you can move back into your bedroom."

All the air whooshed out of John's lungs. He could move back into Caitlan's bedroom? The idea of such a move was incredible. He was so stunned by the involuntary reaction of his body that he couldn't even comment on Sarah's remark.

With a lump the size of a Florida orange in his throat, he managed a terse, "Yes," and retreated toward the loft, climbing the ladder with a vengeance. His mission of mercy was becoming a trial by physical abstinence. He'd be forced to explain their peculiar arrangement to Sarah sooner or later, or her innocent expectations would turn a situation that already was dangerous into a disaster.

In the bedroom Caitlan kept her eyes closed tightly. The thought of John sharing her bed was the agony she'd tried to avoid for days. He was too big, too strong, too confident, and much too tempting. What was she going to do? The idea, once voiced, took on monumental proportions in her mind, and she couldn't stop thinking about the man in her loft.

For the next few days Caitlan paced back and forth in her room. When John was away from the cottage, she sat outside in the sun, hurrying back inside when she heard the sound of his motorcycle approaching. She forced herself to sleep, feed Caity, eat, and sleep some more. She was hibernating, deliberately waiting for him to give up and return to Savannah, but she had to admit that she missed his company. Other than sharing a casual conversation while he stood in the doorway, her bedroom was off-limits.

Trying to find enough physical exercise to keep himself occupied, John joined a local gym where he worked out every day until after lunch. He spent the afternoon hours riding his motorcycle. He'd even taken to stopping by Jeb McGraw's bookstore. One way or another he managed to get through the day and eventually fall asleep at night.

In the bedroom below, Caitlan heard his restless pacing. She was going crazy being cooped up in her bedroom. She knew that she was strong again. Sarah Flanagan had been an extravagance she couldn't have afforded, but she truly didn't need her any longer. She'd apologized when she'd dismissed her earlier that afternoon. She'd have dismissed her sooner were it not for the presence of John Garmon. Sarah had been a barrier between the two of them, and now the barrier had been torn down. Caitlan didn't know how much longer she could hide from the man who was intent on running her life.

"You look tired, John."

John's head gave a sudden lurch as he looked up and saw Caitlan. He'd woken from a midday nap, pulled on a pair of jeans, and made his way to the kitchen with his eyes still half-closed. He squinted, opened his eyes again, then glanced around to take in the silence.

"Where's Florence Nightingale?"

"She's gone, John. I'm sorry if you're angry, but I'm well enough now to take over. We're alone again."

"Are you sure?" John knew his voice was strained. Her announcement had caught him by surprise. The suggestion in her choice of words had floored him. Alone, the two—no—the three of them.

"I'm sure, John. We can manage alone."

His chest was bare, suntanned, and tightly honed from the exercise program he'd thrown himself into. He hadn't shaved for several days, and his hair hadn't been cut. He'd left the Gucci loafers and silk jackets permanently behind as he began to look more and more like a refugee from a motorcycle gang. Gone was the Chairman of the Board from the twenty-first floor. Gone was the cowboy in the white hat. Gone was the take-charge self-assurance that she'd come to resent. He simply stood looking at her with disbelief.

"Alone?"

"John, when are you going back to Savannah?" Her voice was hushed and she could hear an angry gull shrieking at something beyond the deck.

"I can't. Not yet." He managed a crooked smile and shrugged his shoulders. "I can't leave you, my damsel in distress. My mission isn't complete."

"You don't have a mission, really you don't." Her heart went out to this man who was caught up in something he couldn't delegate or walk away from. Her voice softened as she said, "I'll bet you haven't even fed your horse."

"Oh, but I have. A good hero never forgets to feed his horse. How is the dumpling?"

"She's fine. Why haven't you been in to see her?"

"Well, you had Sarah, you didn't need me. And I didn't think you wanted me in your bed . . . room."

Caitlan swallowed hard. It was time she faced him—and her problem—straight on. Didn't want him in her bedroom? That was exactly where she wanted him—in her bedroom, in her bed, in her arms. "Don't be silly," she whispered unsteadily. "Come and see her. She misses you."

She took him by the hand and pulled him inside across the thick carpet to the lace-covered crib. As he looked down at the tiny lump covered with a pale pink square of fabric, the lump began to move. The movement was followed by a bellow of sound that startled John with its urgency.

"What's wrong? More colic?"

"Nope, she just has a very good pair of lungs. Actually, if you don't already know it, she's something of a tyrant. She demands attention. When she's wet, she's a real witch. I think it must be a Garmon genetic characteristic—the demand for instant gratification. This time I think she's hungry."

Caitlan lifted the child and carried her to the rocker by the window. She glanced up at John, smiled, and began to unbutton her blouse. "I need to nurse her, John. If it makes you uncomfortable, you'd better go."

"No." His voice was hoarse. He should have turned his head. He knew how modest Caitlan was, but he was drawn to the scene before him with such intensity that he forgot to breathe. Caitlan's breast with its large dark areola and cherry-colored nipple was the most beautiful thing he'd ever seen. The infant nuzzled for a moment, then grasped it greedily.

Caitlan lifted her eyes and caught John's expression of wonder. He swallowed hard and glanced away. "I'm sorry. I should leave."

"Why? I thought I was the shy one. I guess I expected you to be more sophisticated."

"Me? Sophisticated? No. I'm really just a good old boy. And, yes, I guess it does make me feel peculiar somehow—not uncomfortable, but strange. I don't know why. I suppose I'm more old-fashioned than I realized."

She began to rearrange Caity's blanket to cover herself.

"No, please, don't stop. I like watching you and Caity. You're so calm and accepting. There's something majestic in you, Caitlan Downey, and you make me feel almost spiritual."

"Oh my." She lifted the baby to her shoulder and patted her on the back, then put her back to the breast. "I'm not some spiritual being, John. I'm just an ordinary woman who's had a baby. Don't make it into anything more. I won't even be able to nurse her much longer. Sarah Flanagan says I probably won't have enough milk for more than one good feeding a day."

John took a step closer and looked down at the child. He felt a surge of pride sweep through him, beginning with his knees and working upward until it settled into a warm glow somewhere in the vicinity of his chest. There was something primitive about his reaction to her nursing the child, Jeffrey's child. He wanted to hold her and the child in his arms. He wanted to touch her. He felt himself begin to harden. She incited such conflicting emotions in his body, keeping him constantly on guard and out of step.

"Would you like to hold her?" Caitlan stood, pulled

her blouse closed, and held out the tiny bundle. "You haven't touched her since you got back."

"One night," he started to tell her about the colic attack, then stopped. "You haven't needed me, what with the nurse and all."

He took the baby into his arms. Caity stretched and snuggled close to his bare chest, circling his thumb with her tiny hand. Her soft warm breath touched him, and he felt a fierce stab of protectiveness spear him. She was so small, so fragile, this gift of love Caitlan had offered to his family. John knew, beyond any doubt that, one way or another, she was a part of him. He smiled at Caitlan and slid his arm around her, hugging her as naturally as he had the first time he'd seen her.

They were standing staring into each other's eyes, moved by the unspoken promise of a commitment, a commitment yet to be voiced. Finally he leaned down and touched her lips with his, gently, in tribute, without demand. But he felt the tremor that rippled through her and then through him. He felt the longing, and he knew that she felt it too.

"Thank you, Caitlan," he said simply, "for letting me share this."

"You're welcome, John," she answered, "I understand now that Jeffrey would have wanted you to be here."

Jeffrey. They were back to mentioning Jeffrey, and for a moment John resented his intrusion. He looked down at the child and tried to still the emotions whirling in his lower body. The resentment dissipated, changing into something else that he didn't understand. Caitlan was related to Jeffrey's family first, and they had made a conscious decision to have this child. But Jeffrey and Ann were gone, and sometime soon he had to let Caitlan know that he wanted to claim the child as his own.

"I guess I'll let you take her," he said stiffly. He separated himself from Caitlan, uncurled the baby from his chest, and handed her back to her mother. Trying not to see the confusion on Caitlan's face, he brushed past her, out the door, and down to the beach. Conflicting feelings battled in his mind, accelerating his walk into a jog and finally into a furious run.

What in hell was he doing? Why, he asked himself over and over as he ran, why was he still here? Finally he stumbled, fell across a dune, and stared up into the sky, answering his own questions. Lord help him, he wanted her for himself. How could he explain to her that it had nothing to do with Jeffrey or with the child. Or did it? He didn't know anymore. He only knew that he wanted to make love to her and hear her whisper words of love. John Garmon let out a cry of pained frustration, pulled himself to his feet, and ran again.

Caitlan Downey stood on the deck and watched John tear down the beach as though he were being chased by the hounds of hell. What had she done? She'd hoped that by letting him hold Caity, he'd feel the love the child inspired. She'd hoped that he might be as affected by that love as she had been. She'd hoped that some of that love might spill over on her.

Ever since he'd kissed her the first time, she'd known that the look in his eyes didn't match the words in his mouth. He might have come the first time to get her to sign over voting rights in the stock. But when he'd returned the second time, he'd come because she needed him, because she'd wanted him there. Caitlan had hoped against hope that he might be beginning to need her, too, because she knew with certainty that she was learning to care for the one man in all the world she shouldn't allow herself to love.

Caitlan turned back inside. She had to be strong. She had to consider the child, not herself. But she knew that she couldn't let John Garmon hurt. There had to be another way. *Jeffrey, Ann, you made me promise not to tell, but you couldn't know how much it hurts me not to.*

Six

John Garmon didn't return.

As the afternoon began to slip into early evening Caitlan paced the deck restlessly. Where was he? He'd been gone for over four hours. Finally she turned to the phone and dialed the number of her nearest neighbor, Joe Carlisle.

"I'm looking for a tall, blond man, Joe."

"Will a short blond one do instead?"

She laughed. "No, not today. Did you see a man running down the beach earlier today?"

"Nope, did you lose one?"

"Yes, well, kind of. His name is John Garmon and . . ."

"Garmon? Oh, *that* tall, blond man. Nope. I heard he was back in town, but I haven't seen him. Say, what happened to your Blazer?"

"It isn't mine. It's John's and I loaned it to . . . someone, temporarily," she quickly added.

"John's? He owns a Harley-Davidson, a sports car, and a Blazer? Rich, is he?"

"Yes, I suppose. He's also an executive who takes over and runs people's lives, even when they don't want him to."

"Yeah, like buying you the cottage. Wish I had executive friends like that. Say, are you all right, Caitlan?"

She'd gasped. The cottage? John had bought the beach cottage? "Yes, I'm all right, really I am. Thanks anyway."

But was she? She didn't know. John didn't bulldoze over her, didn't give directions or browbeat her into letting him do things for her. He just quietly and confidently went about making everything easy. It wasn't his control over her life that she couldn't handle. It was the man himself.

John Garmon's touch was becoming addictive. She'd never in her life had such strong feelings for a man before. She clenched her fists and stiffened her body. Her insides had turned into a cement mixer, and she wanted to dash out the door and run after John. She wanted to feel his powerful arms holding her, his lips on hers. Wild conflicting emotions battered her mind and her body. Night after night she'd heard him pacing back and forth overhead, and she'd squirmed uncomfortably in her bed below. She wanted him in that bed with her. What was she going to do? she asked herself.

Half an hour later Joe called back. "Say, I've decided to throw a luau and introduce your man to the locals."

"Oh, I don't know about a party. I mean I haven't been out yet."

"Come on, Caitlan, that kid is four months old. If you don't get back to the world of the living, you're going to turn into a couch potato. I know that you want to be alone with your man, but your friends want to get to know John. Surely you're not hiding him."

"He isn't my man!" She protested vigorously.

"Then what is he?"

"He's . . . well, what I mean is . . . all right, we'll come. That is if he's still here. He has business back in Savannah, and he may have to return before your party. I'll have to let you know." Caitlan hung up the phone.

"What party?"

Caitlan turned and gave a deep sigh of relief. He was back. Sweaty, windblown, his deep tan overlaid with a flush, John Garmon stood in the doorway.

Without a thought she rushed across the room and threw herself into his arms. "Where have you been, John?"

He stiffened, cautiously slipping his arms around her. "Walking, running, chasing away the . . . bad guys. Were you worried?"

"What bad guys, cowboy?" The tone of her voice didn't match the words she said. She reached up and touched his chin, unable to hide the relief in her eyes. She had to touch him.

"The ones who don't know how to trust," he said simply. "When are you going to tell me the truth about the baby?"

"The truth?" Her body went cold and her lips began to tremble. "Why? Does the truth matter?"

"The truth matters. It matters a great deal."

"John Wayne, the flag, and justice for all, huh?

Somehow you never struck me as being the all-American boy."

"I never was. But I never pretended to be. Ah, Caitlan, love, something is happening between us." His fingers softened their grip and began to flex themselves against her skin. She was turning him into whipped cream with her touch. "We can't go on like this. Don't you know that?"

"Yes. But I didn't . . . don't want to." He felt her nipples brushing against his chest and his lower body began to tremble. He ached for her, and he couldn't hold back anymore. He lowered his lips and kissed her.

Caitlan moaned and lifted herself up to reach him. Her lips parted willingly, taking his tongue inside with fervor. Her heart pounded wildly as the roar of passion swept through them. He cupped her bottom in his hands and lifted her from the floor, sliding her against the full, throbbing evidence of his desire. He rubbed her up and down his body, and she felt herself tightening her muscles against the rush of emotion.

"I want you, Caitlan Downey. Lord, I've never wanted a woman so much in my life. I'm going crazy being so close to you without being able to touch you. I want you in my bed. I want to be inside you, holding you, hearing all those little love sounds that you whisper when you're nursing the baby."

"I know," she said. "I know, but we can't let this happen. It isn't real, John. It's only because we're together with the baby. It's an illusion. I don't think you want me for me, John. You want me because you're here and I'm here. Let's not hurt each other."

He stopped all motion and looked down at her

with anguish in his eyes. "I think you're wrong, Caitlan. I'd never hurt you." Caitlan's lips were swollen, her breathing erratic, and she was clinging to him as though she were unable to stand on her own. She might try to fool herself, but he couldn't be wrong about what he was reading in her eyes.

Deeply distressed, Caitlan leaned her face against his chest and tried to still her breathing. "It's me who's at fault. I've never wanted a man before, and I don't know how to keep my feelings from showing. I'm sorry."

"How can you say that? I'm the one who . . . Ah, Caitlan, I've wanted to kiss you forever. I've wanted to touch you—" he slid his hand under her blouse, around her breast, "—here."

Her heart stopped. She held her breath. His touch was like an electric shock sending tremors throughout her body. "What are you doing, John?"

"Just once, Caitlan. I had to touch you. Just once." He lifted her blouse, dropped his head, and took her nipple into his mouth and held it. "I've wanted to do this every time I've watched you nurse Caity. Does that make me some kind of wicked pervert?"

She would have answered him, but her voice had left her at the sensation of his touch. He didn't nuzzle or suck, but simply held her nipple in his mouth as his body pressed against her. Then he groaned, lifted his head, pulled his hand away, and allowed the blouse to drop down and cover her body.

"When I came here, Caitlan, I never had any idea that this would happen. And yet I knew the night on the terrace after the funeral that you were someone special. I didn't have to be the one to come here, but I did. I couldn't stay away. I've spent all afternoon

trying to reach a decision. There is something between us. I'm not sure how smart we are to pursue
it. In fact, we're probably damned stupid, but it's
there, and I think we ought to give it a chance, for
Jeffrey . . . for . . . the baby's sake," he added with
obvious sincerity.

"For the baby's sake?" Caitlan tried to disagree.
She knew that if she agreed to anything for the
baby's sake, it would be a lie. But maybe that was
the answer, she thought. If they gave themselves
enough time, the fire would burn out—if it didn't
consume her first.

"Yes," John went on stiffly. "We ought to call a
truce, try and get to know each other because of the
baby. And sooner or later we'll have to talk about her
too."

"No. I won't discuss the baby, John. Not now, not
ever. I won't give her to you, and I won't let you take
over. I can't. Surely you understand?"

"No, I'll be honest, I don't. But I'll honor your
decision for now."

Caitlan let out a shaky breath. Maybe all wasn't
lost. Maybe if they gave themselves some time they
could work everything out. But she'd promised Jeffrey and Ann that she'd never tell the real truth
about Caity, and nothing could change that.

John wiped his forehead on his sleeve and put his
arms around Ciatlan, pulled her close, and held her.

"Next time I chase the bad guys, remind me to
take my horse," he said with a shaky sigh of relief.
"You smell good."

"Well, you don't." Caitlan drew back and wrinkled
her nose. "Why don't you take a shower while I
prepare dinner?"

John started toward the ladder, stopped, and asked without turning his head. "Dinner together? Just you and me alone without any of your gang?"

"Yes. I don't know how safe we'll be, but we'll be alone."

"How safe do you want your world to be, Caitlan Downey?"

"I don't know. I've never really been alone before, and I never will be, will I? I have Caity."

"And we'll draw the wagons into a circle and hold down the fort." John tucked in his fanny and did a reasonably accurate impression of John Wayne as he strode across the room. "Keep the faith, little pilgrim." He scaled the ladder with a jaunty air, whistling as he walked around overhead.

Caitlan smiled. The tune was becoming familiar. Country music's popularity had taken a meteoric rise ever since they'd danced together at the restaurant.

"I thought John Wayne was a 'Yellow Rose of Texas' man," Caitlan called out from the kitchen.

John leaned dangerously over the loft banister. "He never danced to a she-done-me-wrong tune."

Caitlan looked up and caught her breath. He was wearing a towel across his lower body, a very abbreviated towel that concealed little and promised far too much. "And he never went skinny-dipping in the middle of a cheese soufflé either. Put your pants on, Garmon."

"Ah, shucks, and I thought I was the dessert."

Caitlan mixed the soufflé and put it in to bake. With a happy air she changed into a skirt of lemon-yellow and a soft white sheer blouse. She'd washed her hair earlier and it curled softly around her face. With a little lavender shadow to accent her eyes and some rosy blush, she felt as though she was almost back to normal. Checking her appearance in the mirror, she smiled. John Garmon had never seen her when she wasn't either pregnant or wearing some loose-fitting shift. Now she wanted him to see her as a woman because that's exactly what she felt like.

Sarah Flanagan's final words kept returning to Caitlan as she waited. She'd reminded Caitlan to be certain that he took precautions. It was too soon for her to have another child. In the privacy of her bedroom Caitlan blushed as she realized how close they'd already come to disregarding those directions. Was her desire for John that obvious?

She fed Caity and put her to bed. As she stepped out of the bedroom, she saw John standing on the deck.

Free to watch unobserved, Caitlan let her gaze wander over the man, lovingly taking in the dark burnished gold of his wet hair as it was ruffled by the breeze blowing in from the Gulf. It was Caitlan's favorite time of day when the sky went lavender and the clouds were edged with pink and purple as the sun sank beyond the horizon.

She loved the way he straightened his back and took on that good-guy-sheriff look when he was trying to do the right thing. There was a touch of Jeffrey's goodness in his face, but the strength and determination was all John Lane Garmon III.

They ate the soufflé at the kitchen counter and washed it down with cold milk. John was unusually quiet, answering her questions, discussing the sale of the farm as Caitlan explained Jeffrey's agreement with the court system back in Pretty Springs. "The judge would send him all the runaways under sixteen. He'd keep them for thirty days, then they either went home or to the juvenile welfare center. What we did was fill a need that nobody acknowledged. That's the worst thing about losing the farm."

"I would have thought dealing with delinquents would be pretty tough."

"Really, John. I'm an outlaw, remember? Outlaws relate to kids' problems. Oh, we didn't win them all, but rarely did we lose one to the courts," Caitlan recounted with pride. "Ann was better at dealing with the boys. Surprisingly enough, Jeffrey handled the girls."

"Smart boy, my brother. In fact, that's probably one topic that he and I agreed on." John stood up and took Caitlan's hand. "Let's go out on the deck and watch the sunset."

They stood side by side in comfortable silence, watching the night lower itself in peekaboo fashion across the sky.

"I can understand why you came here," John said finally. "This place is so peaceful. But why did you run away after the funeral?"

"I didn't run—yes, I did. I'll admit it. I thought it was the right thing to do."

"Why, Caitlan? Tell me out here in the dark so that I can't see those great dark eyes of yours get all glazed over and filled with fright."

"Fright? I'm not afraid of you," Caitlan said softly.

"Then prove it. Turn around and face me, and tell me why you really left."

"All right." She turned, leaning her back against the deck rail and resting her weight on her elbows. She looked at him, challenge in her eyes. "Nothing in my life has ever stayed the same. My leaving was just another change. Everything shifted, and I had to find another path. For the first time I was responsible for someone other than myself. So I came back here where I have friends. But you, you're different." She lifted an eyebrow. "What do you want, John?"

On anyone else the lifted eyebrow would have been a tease. On Caitlan, it represented concerned interest. She couldn't know how the slight tilt of the corners of her mouth made her look as though she were doubting him with every breath.

"Oh, don't do this, lady. What do I want? After what happened earlier, you ask me that? I want to lift you in my arms and climb the ladder to the loft. I want . . . Hell, I think you know what I want, but I think I'd better settle for some explanations." He pulled her forward, kissed her lightly on the forehead, and turned her around to watch the sunset. "Talk to me, Ms. Downey, ma'am. I do love to talk. Start with the man down the beach."

"The man down the beach? You mean Joe? He's just a friend. Why?"

"Because he waylaid me as I came back and warned me that the people in Ammacanta County look on a hanging as a routine, end-of-the-month closing of the books—and I'm this month's intended. But they don't mind postponing the hanging if they can exchange it for a wedding. He said to tell you to run up the flag if you need help with me."

"Joe said that?" Caitlan choked back an amused laugh.

"After we shared a soft drink and a few well-chosen insults, I told him that I could be had. He suggested that I put my money where my mouth was and get to it. Pretty bossy friends you have around here."

"John." Caitlan put her hand on his shoulder and turned him so that she could see his face. "John, they don't mean anything by their interference. They just care about me. I was born and raised less than twenty miles from here. Joe and I went to high school together. He's divorced. His little girl comes to stay with him every other weekend. Some weekends he has to work, and she stays with me. In fact . . ."

John groaned. "No, don't tell me, let me guess. This is her weekend for visiting, and she'll be joining us here in the cottage, along with Nurse Flanagan, Tony the postman, Jeb McGraw, and probably even Miss Essie. Wonderful!"

"Why, John, don't you like company?"

"No! I like it when there isn't anybody here but us." He placed his hands on her arms, running his fingertips lightly up and down. "I like it, but it scares me. Let's turn on the radio and find that she-done-me-wrong song. I'd like to dance with you again, Caitlan."

"All right, we dance. But no more talking, please?" Caitlan took the tape player from a shelf in the closet and plugged it into the deck outlet. She clicked in a tape and adjusted the volume. "Outlaw music. Appropriate, don't you think?"

She looped her arms around his neck and began to sway in motion with the tune. Willie Nelson's voice twanged across the open sand as he sang about crying eyes and shattered hearts. This time there was no crowd of onlookers to come between them. This time John rested his chin on the side of Caitlan's head and gave himself over to the primitive feel of having her so close.

"You know, my little outlaw, maybe we ought to open the corral and let some of those friends of yours inside. Maybe being here alone isn't such a smart idea. I can't keep my hands off you, and I think you can feel what just touching you does to me."

"Yes, it's . . ." She grinned and sucked in her breath. "It's . . . awesome." She felt reckless and giddy with the sense of newfound power she held over John.

"Awesome," he said with a growl, and swung her up on the deck rail. "I'll show you awesome. This is awesome." He began to unbutton her blouse very slowly, one button at a time, as if he were waiting for her to stop him. "I just want to look."

"But it's dark," she protested.

"I don't need to see with my eyes." His hands were like feathers lightly brushing her, stroking her with streaks of fire.

"I'm not very big normally. It's having the baby that makes me . . . I mean, it's the milk."

"You're perfect." John tried to hold back, tried to see what he was doing from her point of view, but he couldn't stop himself. Lowering his head, he kissed the top of her breasts, sliding down until he touched her dark, full nipples. He was behaving like some caveman with wild primitive urgings, and he could tell from the way she was trembling that she was sharing the same desire. He was bordering on losing control of himself when Caitlan stopped him.

"John! John!" She was shaking him, pulling away.

"Oh, Lord, I'm sorry, Caitlan. I think you've bewitched me."

"No, it's not that, John. The baby is crying."

He lifted his head and heard the frantic wail of the infant. John stepped back and lifted Caitlan from the rail. She lowered her skirt and dashed inside the cottage, straightening her clothes as she ran.

As Caitlan heated a bottle and changed Caity's diaper, she tried to calm her emotions. By the time she'd finished feeding Caity, she was almost calm, but still so uncertain.

The cottage was dark and John was watching the television when she finally rejoined him.

"Come, look what I found to watch."

Caitlan hung back, trying to stiffen her reserve.

"It's a Gene Autry movie all about smuggling furs across the border from Canada."

Caitlan had been all set to talk some more. They had to discuss what had happened between them on the deck. But every time she decided to get tough, he did something unexpected, something that made her smile. She suspected that underneath all his take-charge airs, John Garmon was just a little boy looking for a best friend to share his interests. Power he could handle. Sex he'd enjoy. But friendship? Maybe they both needed that closeness first.

In the light cast from the television she could see the anticipation on his face as he leaned forward in his seat. In his pale pink polo shirt, washed blue jeans, and scruffy deck shoes, he was beginning to look like a beach bum. He'd left the Chairman-of-the-Board side of his personality so far behind that Caitlan couldn't even remember what he'd acted like.

"Come and sit beside me, Caitlan, and tell me what happens next."

"Is it safe?"

"Would I do something improper in the presence of Gene Autry?"

"I don't know what you'll do, John. No, I'm wrong. I don't know what I'll do. I'm afraid of being alone with you."

He turned to look up at her, and she saw the regret in his gaze. There was pain and a little uncertainty in his face also, the same feelings she was fighting to understand.

"Caitlan," he said quietly, "that won't happen again unless you want it to. I'm being very honest. You and I both know that I ought to get out of here, but I can't. My coming here may have started out as a family responsibility, but the rules changed somewhere along the way. I kiss you because I want to, and every time it happens it surprises the hell out of me."

Caitlan flinched. Honesty. John Garmon spoke of honesty, and she was more dishonest than he'd ever been. She wanted to tell him the truth. "John, I don't know what to say. I realize that you and I could never, I mean even if we should ever want to be more than friends, we couldn't without honesty. I promised Ann that I . . . well, I just can't tell you everything I'd like to. Boy, does that sound dumb."

"Well, at least you're willing to admit that there might be something between us. It's a start. Come and sit down. I won't even try to hold your hand. I'm learning, remember? The cowboy kisses his horse."

Reluctantly Caitlan smiled and moved over to the sofa. She admitted that John was making a crazy kind of sense. She admitted, too, that she wanted to trust him.

He understood her indecision and he gave her a brief respite with his next suggestion. "Why don't you make some popcorn. I'm sure I saw a popper in the cabinet. We'll drink soda and eat popcorn and boo the bad guys."

"Good idea," she managed to reply, shaking her head as she complied. What an incredible man John Garmon was. She didn't believe for one minute that he wouldn't hold her hand. She didn't believe that he wouldn't try to kiss her. And she was lying like a rug on the floor if she told herself that she didn't want him to.

Caitlan poured oil in the popper and let it heat while she gathered glasses and bowls, adding the corn when the oil was hot enough. Soon the cottage was filled with a warm buttery smell. Filling the bowl with the popped corn and the glasses with ice and soda, she carried them to the coffee table.

"Look at the bad guy. He's Pierre LeBeau. He's trying to keep the country from becoming civilized."

Caitlan sank down into the thick cushions of the couch and turned her attention to the movie. The film was in black and white, enhancing the beauty of a scene in a snow-covered wood.

John took a hand full of popcorn and held it while he watched. "I can see why you like these old movies."

Caitlan took a deep sip of soda and said, "You know who the hero is, and you know he'll win. No gray characters there, only black and white."

"Ah, shucks. You mean the bad guy never repents?"

"Oh, sure. But you always knew from the start that the bad guy wasn't really bad. He was either protecting someone he loved or he was honestly mistaken."

Protecting someone he loved, or honestly mistaken. Like me?" John asked seriously.

Caitlan gave him a searching look. "You're not a bad guy. Of course, you're not necessarily the good guy either. I think you're a little of both. Maybe that's why you run the company for your mother and ride motorcycles for yourself. Maybe you're the man with the white hat riding a black horse. Maybe you're not sure what you want to be when you grow up."

"Maybe I'm not." John thought about what she'd said as the chase scene on the television built to a climax. Was he a good guy or a bad guy? "Look here, outlaw," he began in his best Texas drawl, "lighten up. This conversation is getting too deep for me. I'm just a guy who's learning to like old movies and fragile-looking ladies with dark eyes."

Caitlan threw her hand across her eyes and gasped convincingly. "Don't call me an outlaw, sir. An outlaw is person who is wanted by the law. I declare, 'm just a poor damsel in distress." She sat up, dropped her melodramatic pose, and added softly, "I'm simply a woman who left a past she couldn't change for a future she could. I make my own decisions, John, and I look for rainbows. I don't need much to make me happy."

"Maybe another definition for an outlaw is a fugitive. Maybe, in a crazy kind of way, that's what we both are, Caitlan Downey." John placed his glass on the table and faced her.

"Fugitive? Not anymore." A fleeting shadow fur-

rowed her brow and she shook her head. "Perhaps
came back here to face my own bad guys. Only i
isn't the same. They've all gone away—my mother
Ann, Jeffrey. I can't tell anymore who wears th
white hat."

"Do you miss them?"

"Terribly. But I'm good at missing people. First
lost my mother. Well, she was there but she was
only a shell. I didn't know my father. My mother had
a number of male friends. When the last one left
she couldn't cope. She turned bitter and dried up
inside. I think that when she punished Ann and
me, she was punishing herself."

"I'm sorry, darling." John took her hand, wishing
he could hold her in his arms.

"She didn't understand why Ann and I wanted to
leave this place," Caitlan continued, unaware that
she'd taken John's hand and was gripping it tightly
"but Ann needed to grow and to learn about the
world, and she needed me—my mother didn't. So
one day we took off. I think I might have been wrong
about my mother. She died before I realized how
hard it was for her to let us know how she felt. I
don't ever want to keep my feelings bottled up inside." But she had to, she thought.

Caitlan didn't know why she'd told him so much.
She'd never talked so much about her past, not even
to Jeffrey. Even now she couldn't describe the great
need she felt, the need to belong, to be needed by
those around her. When she did something for somebody else, she was doing it for her mother. But it
was never quite enough.

"I think I understand, Caitlan. I had a father. But

he was such a shadow of a man that I resented his being there almost as much as you resented not having a father. He always was away when I was growing up. He was a marine. He served in Korea. He was decorated as a hero, but then something happened. He retired from military life and came home an empty, vacant man. I never knew why he was so empty."

"How sad for your mother."

"She never understood him either. He rejected her, and she found other ways to find fulfillment. But I'm sure she was very hurt. I suppose that's why I've tried to follow her wishes. She's lost so much in her life."

"Perhaps our mothers were more alike than we know," Caitlan said. She looked down at the tight clasp she had on John's hand and released it with an embarrassed motion.

"But your mother is gone, Caitlan, so why come back here? You'd made a life in Pretty Springs. I would have thought you would have stayed there."

"I'm not sure. Pretty Springs was Ann and Jeffrey's home. I suppose I'd made myself an extension of them, and I needed to make a new start, my own new start. So here I am. I like it here. I belong. Why haven't you split from the candy company?"

"I don't know. I understand now why Mother took over. I never knew how painful her life must have been. First she lost my father, then Jeffrey. I couldn't add to her burdens."

"You are truly a kind man, John Garmon."

"Then," he went on, "when she learned that Jeffrey was married she wanted a grandchild more than anything in the world. She wanted Jeffrey and Ann to be a part of the family, but she didn't know how to tell them. Expressing love is something she's never found easy. I wasn't remotely interested in marriage at the time, so your sister was her only hope. When she lost Jeffrey and Ann, her dream of grandchildren was taken away from her."

John leaned forward, turning his gaze away from her to the movie. "What about you, Caitlan," he asked casually, "wouldn't you like to fill in that gap?"

"What, be her grandchild?" she said in a feeble attempt at humor. "Oh, I'm too old. Besides," Caitlan said in a rush, "being a Garmon doesn't leave room for a person to be anything else, does it?"

A peculiar smile etched itself across John's face. "Nope, being a Garmon is a full-time job. I guess any smart person would turn down that kind of job. It's probably much smarter to be an outlaw," he said.

"That's me," she agreed quietly. That's us, she wanted to say, two refugees from the past who've come together and don't know how to act.

"So, we need new rules—law and order. You've come to the right place, outlaw. I've always wanted to make a citizen's arrest. Hold out your hands," he said.

"Darn, and I thought you promised no holding hands."

"I lied. Maybe I ought to turn in my white hat."

The mood lightened as Caitlan went along with John's lighthearted banter.

"Not on your life, John Garmon. You're my champion, I wouldn't have it any other way. There just aren't any real heroes around. You're probably the last."

Without her knowing how it had happened, John's arm came across her shoulder, and they snuggled back on the couch to watch the movie. The sound of the churning waves outside the cottage was an echo of the crashing emotions vibrating within the two people inside. They'd revealed too much, and neither one knew how to let go of their private uncertainties. They sat together, yet each held back.

A storm was blowing in. As the surf began to swell and roar, the wind made a high-pitched whining noise, and Caitlan thought that she could almost make out the frightened whinny of a horse outside. At last she began to relax. John's arm became her security, and she felt his own tension melt away as they sat in the darkness.

She was safe, safer than she'd felt in a very long time. No matter what reservations she had about the man holding her, she knew that he was a good man. And she knew, too, that he really cared. She never did like storms. When the lightning struck and the rain swept over the house, they remained close and snug, not talking, simply enjoying being together.

The next morning John found Tony the postman at the breakfast table. He'd brought Caity a rattle. For lunch Nurse Ratched from the doctor's office joined them. Later that afternoon one of the Carnival Strip police officers stuck his head in to see the baby. He came empty-handed, offering his police car as a taxi if Caitlan needed it.

John's refusal wasn't at all gracious. When Caitlan wasn't entertaining guests, she was writing letters, answering the phone, and cooking meals for the guests she anticipated. As soon as they'd eaten Caitlan excused herself and went to her room, pleading exhaustion. After three days spent with assorted friends and neighbors who'd casually dropped by John began to get the picture.

The fourth day Miss Essie brought over a casserole and crocheted booties for Caity. When John heard Caitlan on the phone cajoling Jeb McGraw into coming for supper, he knew it was time for a showdown.

He waited until after lunch when they were sitting on the deck sipping iced tea.

"Okay, Caitlan, call off your gang. I give you my word, you don't need protection from me."

"You must be joking, John. I don't think I need protection from you." She flipped the dark glasses she'd pushed up on her head down to cover her eyes. She was afraid he'd see the truth reflected there. It wasn't him she was afraid of. It was herself.

"What about Jeb McGraw? Should I be prepared for a lie detector test when he arrives?"

"No, Jeb isn't coming."

"Really, Why?"

"He thinks we ought to be alone."

A noisy sea gull crossed the sky and screamed out in the silence.

"Well, now," John finally said, "I guess that means I ought to take up reading. I like a man who tells it like it is. Jeb McGraw is a man who speaks my language."

Caitlan stood up and went inside, calling over her shoulder, "Don't get too happy, cowboy, he's coming next week instead."

John groaned out loud and leaned back under the umbrella. He was doomed. So far he'd kept Caitlan from going back to work. He'd stocked the kitchen with groceries, which she'd used to feed her guests. She'd been pleasant company. He'd thought they were becoming friends, but she'd retreated behind a wall of outsiders. Between her friends, and the baby, he might never have another minute alone with her, he thought. Maybe he ought to be glad.

He wasn't.

Seven

Somehow Caitlan and John were able to establish a routine that bordered on being normal. The tension was there, both of them knew it. It grew steadily as they went about the business of coexisting within an unacknowledged framework of mutual awareness. It was as if they had put themselves on hold.

Between visitors Caitlan arranged short trips with John—normal things, like shopping for groceries, stopping by the cleaners, going for drives in the new car, anything to keep them from being alone in the cottage. John seemed to have pulled back. He didn't try to kiss her. In fact his lack of touching was becoming as sexual as his previous attention had been frustrating. By the next week Caitlan's temper had grown short. After breaking two cups she gave up drinking coffee. When she snapped at Caity unnecessarily, she knew the time had come to make some new arrangements.

The morning they went for the baby's checkup,

Caitlan insisted that John wait outside. "I'd rather go in alone, John."

"Why? I'm concerned about Caity's health."

"Don't be!" Caitlan said, then wished she hadn't.

"But she is my niece, and I want to talk to the doctor about supplementing her formula with solid food. I think it's time."

"Who appointed you Mother of the Year? I'll be the one to ask," Caitlan insisted. She didn't know how to tell John that it wasn't his place to be concerned. This was a matter to be decided between the baby's mother and the doctor. He simply couldn't go on involving himself in her life. He'd be gone soon enough, she guessed, and he had to learn that she'd be the one making the decisions. It was becoming too easy to make him a part of the family. The time was approaching when he'd leave, and she didn't know what would happen to Caity when he was gone.

"At least I've done a little research on parenting. Have you?"

John realized they'd begun to snipe at each other unnecessarily. She was making him deviate from his normal way of handling people, and he didn't like his reactions. He didn't like the pain that flashed in Caitlan's eyes at his remark. An insensitive clod was what he was becoming. "I'm sorry I said that, Caitlan. You know that I didn't mean to imply that you—"

"I don't know what you meant, but I'm going inside and you're staying outside. If I have to call Lieutenant Kelly, I'll do it. You wait here!" She slid out of the car, removed Caity from the car seat, and slammed the door behind them. She knew she'd startled John with her insistence, but she was grateful that he hadn't followed.

When the doctor insisted on examining her as well, Caitlan was glad John had waited outside. "Your blood pressure is a little high," he observed with a frown.

"Tell me about it," Caitlan murmured under her breath.

"But on the whole, I'm very pleased with your progress, Caitlan. For all practical purposes you're back to your old self. You can think about going back to work, resuming all your normal activities, including . . ." he paused and lifted a skeptical eyebrow ". . . sex. However, I would advise taking proper precautions to avoid pregnancy anytime soon."

"Sex?" Caitlan's heart took a sudden lurch. She thought of John, John who made no apologies for wanting her, whose very touch turned her to melted butter inside. If her blood pressure had been high before, it went into orbit. She only nodded and gave a weak, high-pitched yes.

"Caity is doing very well also," Dr. Eubanks reported with great satisfaction. "I've notified the doctors in Atlanta who performed the procedure. They're very excited and want to include you as a case history in a textbook they're compiling."

"No! They can't. I mean they knew from the beginning that this was to be kept confidential. I made a promise to my sister and brother-in-law that nobody else would ever know about this conception. I can't break my word and give my permission."

A pained look furrowed the doctor's face. "Yes, and I'm dreadfully sorry that I told your brother-in-law. I thought when he came to the hospital that morning that he was Caity's father. I didn't know that your sister and his brother had been killed. Otherwise I would never have betrayed a confidence. I hope I didn't make it too difficult for you."

Told your brother-in-law. Caitlan felt the earth move beneath her feet. "You mean John Garmon knew about Caity's conception all along?" She was stunned. Her breathing turned shallow and her head began to spin.

John had known about the baby being Jeffrey's and *Ann's* for the last month and he hadn't said anything. What was he planning? Did he intend to wait until the time was right and make a bid to claim her baby as Mettie Garmon's grandchild? He couldn't do that, could he? she wondered.

"No!" She stood up and clasped the child. "I won't allow him to take her!"

Dr. Eubanks stood up and cleared his throat dramatically, "Is he trying to make trouble for you, Caitlan? I was under the impression that he . . . that you and he . . ."

"No," she admitted hoarsely. "He hasn't done anything, not really. I mean he's driving me crazy, but he hasn't made a move to claim Caity. I mean I've made certain that he didn't have a chance. But knowing how badly his mother wants a grandchild, I expect him to."

"Would you like me to talk to him, Caitlan?" The doctor ran his finger around the collar of his shirt nervously. Perspiration was beading up on his forehead. "I mean, I don't really have time to get into some long, drawn-out court trial. You understand, don't you?"

"There won't be any court trial," she promised. "Mr. Garmon is leaving—soon." Caitlan walked slowly down the corridor and out into the waiting room, forcing herself to relax and cover her feelings. Anger would only make her lose control, and she was going to need a great deal of control to deal with the Garmons.

Inside the waiting room, John came to his feet with a smile of pleasure spread across his lips. Lordy, she thought, he was good-looking, gentle—all in all the kind of man any woman would give her right arm for. She might consider giving up her right arm, but she had no intention of giving up her baby. Caity was hers. She'd borne her, nursed her, loved her.

When John attempted to take Caity from her arms, Caitlan stiffened. When the baby opened her eyes and smiled in joy at the big blond man, Caitlan gave her up reluctantly. What was the right thing to do? She and Ann had never known their father. Their lives might have been different if they hadn't been illegitimate. Certainly the world had changed. Caity wouldn't have the same obstacles to overcome that she and Ann had. Yet Ann had sworn her to secrecy, without realizing that they were recreating the same situation for little Caity that they'd endured as children.

She bit back the sudden bitterness of her thoughts and moved quickly to the car. They'd known they were on shaky ground when they'd made the decision for Caitlan to carry the child for Ann. Ann had lost four babies and each loss had taken a little more out of her. Jeffrey hadn't wanted to put her through such heartbreak again.

The in vitro procedure had been Caitlan's idea and they'd finally agreed, but they'd wanted to avoid the publicity involved. The child would be a Garmon, and in Georgia the Garmons' lives were open books. Between the press and the powerful Mettie Garmon, the pregnancy would have been a nightmare. So would a court case be now. She'd postpone any discussion of the situation until she'd had time to think.

"What's wrong, Caitlan?"

"Nothing, John. I'm just trying to get my plans made. The doctor said that I'm ready to resume normal activities, which means I'm going back to work. You can go back to Savannah."

"You'd leave Caity?"

"For no longer than I have to. I'll do private-duty nursing. As much as possible, I'll take her along."

"I see."

"No, you don't," Caitlan said steadily. "You've been playing a game here. In a way we both have, from the start. I've tried to allow you to see who I am, but this is my life and I have to make my own way in it. We aren't a family, John. You've fulfilled your duty to your brother and your mother. The stocks are mine, but the control is yours. Caity and I are going to have to get along without you. The time has come for you to go."

John's lips tightened and he drove with unusual caution. "I see."

"You're driving me crazy, John. I've got to get on with my life—alone."

"I can't leave you, Caitlan. I never did the right thing for Jeffrey when he was alive. I have to see this through."

A dry wind swept inside the car and wrapped them in the summer heat. John flipped on the air conditioner and soon the car was cool. As they drove away from the Strip the traffic died down, and they were alone on the road when they reached the tip of the beach. Caitlan could see people moving about inside the cottages that had been deserted through the spring months. The part-time residents were returning to the sun the way the swallows return to Capistrano.

"Soon I'll have to find new quarters," she began, waiting for his contradiction. "The owners of the cottage will be arriving."

"That won't be necessary, Caitlan. You don't have to leave the cottage if that's where you want to stay." He knew that he was taking a calculated risk. He was accustomed to taking risks, but this time the potential for failure was personal. This time he was being forced to reveal a part of himself that he wasn't certain he understood.

"What do you mean?" Caitlan shifted the baby, who'd fallen asleep.

Concentrating on his driving, John's brow wrinkled, his hands tightened on the wheel. "The cottage is yours."

"What do you mean, mine?"

"You know by now that I tend to take charge. The first day, when I bought the television and the car, I bought the cottage too. It's in your name. You and Caity can stay there forever—if that's what you want."

The wind stopped. The world outside the car seemed to go into some kind of slow motion. Caitlan took short, deep breaths and tried to gather her thoughts. Finally, at last he'd been honest with her, she thought.

"Why, John? Why did you do that without asking me? Didn't it occur to you that such a big decision might be something I'd like a say in?"

"I'm sorry, Caitlan. At the time I thought that if I provided for you as Jeffrey had asked me to, it would be easier to regain control of the stock. I didn't understand . . . the situation." John turned the car off the road and down into the drive to the house. He cut off the engine and stared ahead without looking at her.

"That's what I mean, John. This is my life. I'll make my own decisions." Caitlan began to gather up Caity's diaper bag and her purse.

"Here, let me take that." John reached across her to take the bag, brushing her arm and pulling back with a startled jerk.

"No! I'll do it." She slid out of the car and went to the door, waiting stiffly for John to unlock the locks that he'd had installed. She took Caity into the bedroom, laid her on the bed that John had provided, and glanced out of the window of the cottage that John had bought. He'd taken care of everything, just as Jeffrey had asked. John Garmon was a good son and a good brother. She felt a lump lodge in her throat, and she wanted to scream in pure frustration.

What hurt the most was that they'd felt right together, once they called the truce and put their sexual tension behind them. For a time they'd spent nice quiet evenings together, had lively discussions about politics, books, movies, and the world in general. They'd gotten to know each other very well.

Like strangers who meet once and never meet again, they'd bared their most intimate secrets. She'd told John about her mother and her feelings of inadequacy that stemmed from her illegitimacy. John had talked about his father and his uncertainties about himself as a man. Then something had happened to change things. They'd become a man and woman with strong feelings for each other, and neither had been ready for that.

At last she went in search of John. The problem couldn't be avoided any longer. He'd come charging in, not wearing a white hat as she'd joked, but wearing a mask, just like her own. Now they were about to pull them off and expose their true faces.

John was standing in front of the sliding glass doors looking out over the brilliant blue-green Gulf waters. He heard her and turned, holding up his hand to stop her.

"No, Caitlan. Don't say anything. We both knew that it had to end. But I want us to have this last day and night together—for us. We'll get Danni to watch the dumpling, we'll spend the afternoon together, go to Joe's party tonight, and then we'll talk. For just one day we'll put aside all our reservations and be ourselves. Then I'll leave, if that's still what you want. Please?"

Standing there with the sun behind him, John's face was in the shadows. She couldn't tell what he was feeling. But she could hear the pain in his voice. He knew that it was over, but he was asking for one last night. Could she refuse him after what he'd done to help her? No, she decided with relief. She'd been given a reprieve, one last day and night ogether. Her heart lurched wildly. One more day and night with John Garmon, without pretense. She could give him that. She could give herself the same because she knew it was the end.

Simply said, her answer was, "Yes."

An hour later they were riding down the beach on John's motorcycle. Her arms wrapped around John's chest, her head resting against John' shoulder, she could feel and smell him with an intimacy that made her slightly mad with excitement. This was their day and she meant to enjoy it, savor the memories to keep with her after he'd gone.

They headed for the amusement rides on the Strip. They rode the Ferris wheel, the bumper cars. She found out that John loved cotton candy. He bought popcorn and ice cream for her. They held hands and laughed. He put his arms around her and kissed her in the house of mirrors, and they laughed at the reflection of the giant-sized man and the midget woman. She told herself that they were two children playing. The day was make-believe, and she was entitled to be Cinderella for once in her life.

Inside the tunnel of love, the kiss he gave her wasn't light and the touch of his hand on her breast was quick, almost accidental. But it set off a glow inside her that seemed to burn brighter with every minute they were together.

Late afternoon found them walking arm and arm on a secluded beach, oblivious to the sun beaming down. John Garmon had been transformed from the family messenger boy, the take-charge executive, into a long-haired beach bum with laughing eyes and loving lips. When he stopped and drew her into his arms, she went willingly.

A hot breeze buffeted her and blew away any qualms she might have been ready to voice. She lifted her head to meet his kiss. Passion flared, hot and intense, and they meshed into each other greedily. Her hands slid underneath his shirt, and she explored the tense muscles of his back, then slid her hands around to the soft mat of hair on his chest, finally rimming his button-hard nipples with her fingertips, setting off spasms with her touch.

In return his hand cupped her against him while he ripped her shirt from the band of her skirt, urgently seeking access to her breasts.

She moaned, feeling the strength drain from her legs as her body turned into fiery liquid. When he pressed her against him, she shuddered at the intense pleasure spreading over every inch of her. She was aching with desire, wanting him with every part of her, trembling uncontrollably when he pulled his mouth away and gazed down at her in awe.

She leaned back, taking in the glazed look of desire in his eyes, his shallow breathing, and the unmistakable throb of him against her. It would be so easy for her to give in to what they both wanted, to fall to the sand and let him love her just once to last for all her life. She wanted to lift his shirt over his head, slide his slacks down his body, and feel his bare skin against her own.

"Let's go home, Caitlan," he said hoarsely. "I want to make love to you. I've never wanted anything as much in my life."

"I'd be lying," she whispered as steadily as she could, "if I told you I didn't want you too. But . . . but . . ."

He kissed her words away, squeezed her against him once more. Then he let her slide down his body until her feet touched the sand. Caitlan's knees trembled as if they'd been asleep. He kept one hand on her back, gently, comfortingly as they made their way to the motorcycle.

All the way back to the cottage, Caitlan leaned against him, holding him close, threading her fingers through the mat of soft hair on his chest. Once, at the stoplight, he turned his head and kissed her lightly. "There should be a law that men wear only sweatpants when they ride on a motorcycle with a woman."

"Why?" she asked innocently.

"Anything with a zipper is potentially dangerous while sitting down."

"I'm a nurse. Can I do anything to help?" She flexed her fingers beneath his shirt and began to inch downward, feeling the sudden expansion of his chest as he took a deep breath.

"Stop that, woman. Even your friend Kelly wouldn't approve of what you're doing to a man who's unable to defend himself."

"I'm only trying to determine the extent of the problem, John. I've been trained to take care of emergencies."

When the light changed, John accelerated and they roared off down the street. "Medically speaking, Nurse Goodbody, if you put your hands any further down, the situation could accelerate into a full-scale disaster. You're dangerous, Caitlan Garmon. But, Lord, how I . . ."

The last part of his answer was swept away by the

wind, but not before she heard enough to know that he hadn't called her Downey.

All day the question of Caity and the truth of her parentage had been pushed aside. Both of them had been content to let it wait. All day they'd played with an intensity brought on by the knowledge that their being together would soon end. Now as they drove back to the cottage, each was aware that they only had a few hours left before they had to face the inevitable.

"Shall we shower and dress for Joe's luau?" Caitlan dropped her purse on the counter and stood in the darkened living room.

"Do we have to go?" He'd come up behind her. His hands slid around her waist, and he pulled her against him, burying his nose in her hair. "You smell like the sea."

Her breath came at a rapid pace. She couldn't move. The ache that had simmered just below the surface for several hours began to spread, and her heart beat so hard, she knew he could hear it. No! She couldn't let him make love to her. That would be wrong, the practical part of her insisted. While another part of her, the deepest, most emotional inner self whispered, Yes!

His hands went up, moving beneath the soft, worn T-shirt she was wearing to rest on her breasts.

"I can't go to bed with you, John," she whispered unsteadily. "I've never done that kind of thing before. And there's too much at stake. It isn't just you and me we have to consider. It involves Jeffrey and Ann, your mother . . . Caity." Her hands clenched and unclenched as she felt the ache spread.

"Not tonight, Caitlan. Tonight there's only John and Caitlan, here in this time and this place. Let me love you, Caitlan."

"Why, John?"

"No whys. No yesterdays or tomorrows. Just you and I, and what we feel."

"I could tell you that we're playing a dangerous game, John Garmon." Her voice was low and beguiling.

"And I'd tell you that I know it, and it's no game. Then you'd ask why." he pressed himself against her, unable to control the involuntary motion of his body.

"And you'd give me some logical reason that I'd believe because I want you," she whispered, in a daze as she realized that her shirt and bra were gone. One hand was sliding inside the belt of her shorts in front, and the other peeling the fabric away from her body in the rear. She was being assaulted with such wonderful sensations of heat and desire that she could no longer hold back.

As the shorts and panties dropped to her feet, she gasped and whirled around. She wanted no barrier between them. John groaned as she unbuttoned his shirt. He stood, not touching her, as she removed his shirt, unzipped his pants, and worked her fingers inside. Wickedly she circled his body with a slow, maddening motion, cupping his rear, sliding his briefs and trousers down an inch at a time. Caitlan had never touched a man intimately. She'd never wanted to know a man's body—until now. An inch away from the hard, throbbing part of him that pulsated against her stomach, she hesitated.

"Touch me, Caitlan," he whispered hoarsely. "I want to feel your hands on me."

He took her face in his hands and kissed her, turning her shyness into courage. As she touched him, his tongue teased at her lips, parting them gently, insistently until she held the length of him in her hands. Then his tongue invaded the moist heat of her mouth, and he moved himself in her grasp. He moved once, moaned, and tensed his body muscles into stillness again—but Caitlan couldn't comply. As his tongue assaulted her, she leaned against him, tugging at him with an urgency she wouldn't control.

"Not so fast," he whispered as he tore himself away from her, taking her hands in his as he tried unsuccessfully to stop his panting. He felt her trembling, felt her dismay, and understood what she was feeling. "We have all night. I don't want to frighten you. I have to—Ah, hell, I can't wait either, Caitlan." He went down on his knees, pulling her to the carpet with him, and covered her with his body. Supported by his elbows and his knees, he rubbed himself against her without entering her. His insistent body found the warm moist heat of her and he felt her opening herself to him. His pace was slow as he waited for her body to be completely ready. She was so small, so lovely, and he wanted to sink himself into her with an urgency he'd never known.

He heard the soft mewing cries that he'd dreamed of. Her fingertips dug into his back as she arched against him, and he couldn't wait any longer. With a slow, gentle motion he moved inside her, feeling her body open to receive him as if they'd been custom-designed to match. He forced himself to move very slowly, holding back as he encountered the slightest suggestion of a barrier.

"Oh!" she cried out, and shifted her legs to fit herself against him. "Oh, John."

He was lost as the boiling emotion that they'd suppressed for so long gave way to the mysterious, overwhelming hunger of desire. Caitlan was conscious only of the feel of his mouth on her lips and the curious sucking sound of their bodies as they came together, parted in a whisper, and came together again. And then it began, the rising tide of heat that rolled over her, racked her body with spasms of pure delight and catapulted her beyond understanding. John was kissing her, touching her, murmuring little words of love as he trembled with some powerful force that slowly accelerated his movements with a wild abandon, joining them together forever.

John arched himself and filled her with an inner heat. She gasped and let the last delicious ripples of release spread over her body. Then she was conscious once more of John still inside her, holding himself over her, kissing her tenderly.

She opened her eyes shyly to meet the puzzled expression on John's face, an expression filled with both tenderness and concern.

"Did I hurt you, darling?"

Darling? He'd called her darling, she realized.

"Am I too heavy? Do you want me to move?"

John kissed her eyes, her cheeks, behind her ears, and then he found her breasts. When he closed his mouth over her nipple, he felt the shudder deep inside of her answer his question with an involuntary tightening that brought his own desire to flame once more. But even as he acknowledged the answer she was giving, he was aware of the unfamiliar sensation he'd encountered. There was a virginal tightness about her that he recognized in belated surprise.

"Caitlan," he whispered. "Caitlan, love, I'm going to ask you a question and I need very much to have you answer it."

His tone alerted her, and she forced herself to push aside the delicious sensation beginning again inside her and concentrated on his voice. "John Garmon," her voice floated dreamily, "this may come as a surprise to you, but I like you better as the outlaw. Couldn't you send the Chairman of the Board back to the twenty-first floor? This is one time I don't want to be rescued."

"This is your first time, isn't it?"

"Probably." She wriggled her body beneath him and was rewarded when the part of John still throbbing inside of her tightened. "I'm usually the rescuer."

"I mean to make love," he insisted, trying to still the gentle undulation that was beginning between them. "I'm the first?"

"Yes. Does it matter?"

"Oh, yes!" His kisses were different now, gentle, wondrous, loving touches that turned quickly into a demand that neither of them tried to control. His body was new and exciting to her, and she explored and examined every part of him. She buried her face in the hair of his chest, running her fingers up and down his firm rib cage and stomach as he continued to hold himself stiffly over her.

With a roar John gave in to the wonder of the feeling she'd fanned to new life with her touch. He encased himself into the tight, moist cocoon into which he fitted so perfectly. The journey was longer this time, building like the storm at sea to a shattering crescendo that carried them past the moment into eternity.

Afterward John slid over her and pulled her into his arms. For once he didn't want to talk. Tired and content, he found her breast and held it until he slept.

Caitlan lay curled against him, feeling the wonderful sensations of being close to a man, of being loved and satisfied by a man—a man she loved in return. How was it possible that she'd fallen in love with John Garmon? What was it about him that singled him out from all the other men she'd ever known? She wasn't certain that she liked him. She definitely didn't approve of his bulldozer approach. But every day he stayed with her she lost more of herself. She didn't want him in her life, but he'd forced his presence on her, and he'd taught her what loving a man could be like. It hadn't mattered before, but now she'd have to learn how to live without love when he was gone. Gone—the thought caught at her heart. It was the way it had to be, but tonight was theirs and she wouldn't let tomorrow intrude.

She raised herself on one elbow, and in the half-darkness she gazed down at him. He was beautiful, a blond Viking who made her body shiver when she looked at him. She was a nurse. She'd seen naked men before, bathed their bodies. But he was different. He was John. She thought of Caity and wished that she was their child.

She gasped. For all she knew they could have created a new life. When the doctor had said that she could resume having sexual relations, she hadn't commented. She'd been too embarrassed to admit that she'd never had any sexual experiences. They hadn't taken any precautions. John hadn't realized that they'd needed to. She sighed deeply. She was a nurse and she should have known better than to take such risks. Quickly she calculated and let out a sigh of relief. If timing could be relied upon, she'd be safe. Did she want to be safe? . . .

John pulled her back into his embrace. With a wicked sigh, Caitlan gave in to the urge to touch him and placed her fingers around his manhood. Her touch brought an instant quiver of response and she felt him harden.

"You know, I'm fifteen years past my peak," he whispered in her ear. "Theoretically, I might not be able to make love to you three times in an hour."

"What?" Caitlan withdrew her hand, embarrassed that she'd been caught.

"But tonight theories don't come into play. Tonight I'm a man of action." And he was.

Caitlan forgot her embarrassment. She forgot her concern about tomorrow. She forgot everything but the man who filled her with a joy that only matched her zest for life.

The luau was in full progress before Caitlan and John arrived. Caitlan didn't even try to hide her newfound joy. She knew it showed. Every loving touch of John's hands on her body gave her away, and her need to touch him in return was more than she could hide. This was her night with John and her friends. She wanted to be near the people who would have to help her get through her loss when he was gone. For one night, Caitlan was a woman in love.

Eight

"So, when are you leaving?" Joe asked as he collapsed into the sand beside Caitlan, pressing a tall ice-filled glass of lemon-spiced tea into her hand.

"Leaving?" Caitlan took a sip of the tea and repeated his question. "Is the party over?"

She was watching John, who'd been cajoled into joining the limbo dance taking place on the beach. John had seriously studied the gyrations of the dancer before him as she slithered beneath the limbo pole. Giving Caitlan a thumbs-up signal he began a crablike motion that might have taken him beneath the bar except for a last-minute sweep of the hand. John collapsed into the sand as the group clapped their hands in reward for his good-natured attempt.

Caitlan joined in the merry applause. John Garmon, prostrating himself in the sand after a foiled attempt at an idiotic dance—he'd come a long way, she decided. Even the Gucci loafers had disappeared, exchanged for a pair of scruffy docksiders. The silk jacket had been permanently replaced by an *Everybody Strips at the Carnival* T-shirt.

Joe smiled sadly. "I think so, love. For you and me. I've lost you, babe. You've changed."

"Changed? Joe, what do you mean?" Caitlan drew her gaze away from the dancers and studied her old friend.

"You're different, Caitlan. Look at you. Your eyes have that soft, dreamy expression of a woman in love."

"Does it show, Joe?"

"It's written all over both of you. Garmon's in cutoffs acting like one of us. And if that isn't enough, for the first time since I've known you, you're wearing something totally feminine. You look like a movie star from the forties, about to be sacrificed to the god of some Polynesian volcano. You can't keep your eyes off each other."

Caitlan glanced down at the soft lavender print sarong that hugged her slender body. She'd found it on her bed when she came out of the shower—another gift from John. When they'd started out the door, he'd taken a single white orchid from the refrigerator and pushed it behind her left ear.

"That's to show those turkeys at the party that you're spoken for." He'd grinned and kissed her. Their departure had been delayed while he showed her how the native women tied their sarongs properly. His insistence that she practice resulted in a second delay, and the party was in full progress when they arrived sated and shining with the unmistakable aura of just having made love.

"He is a good man, Caitlan. We'll miss you, but you're doing the right thing."

"Miss me? What do you mean? I'm not going anywhere."

A confused expression came over Joe's face. "But I thought . . . John said . . . never mind," he managed, shaking his head, "I probably misunderstood him this afternoon."

John stopped to talk with Jeb and his date. The music on the tape player changed from the frenzied beat of the limbo music to the familiar sound of one of Elvis Presley's biggest hits, "Blue Hawaii." Before Caitlan could question Joe further, John had left Jeb and walked back to Caitlan, holding out his hand to lift her into his embrace.

"Excuse me, Joe, I want to dance with . . . my woman."

"In the sand?" Caitlan made a half-hearted protest and went into his arms.

"Well, the natives do it. It's called the hula."

"Not together."

"It's no fun alone." He kissed her beside her ear, and she felt the flutter of his heart as she pressed herself willingly against him.

"Am I to be sacrificed to the gods?" Caitlan slid her arms around his neck and followed the sensual motions he was making with his body.

He looked startled for a moment, placed his hands on her hips, and directed her motions so that they were creating a ritual as old as time. Her hands never stopped touching him as they moved across his face, his eyes, his mouth.

Caitlan's hair brushed against John's chest, tantalizing him. He groaned. "Where'd you learn to do this, lady?"

"Ann and I once took a class in hula and other

exotic dances. Ann was the dancer. I'm no good. The object is to tell the story without touching your partner. I'm a failure. I flunked."

"Failure, hell, darling." It was also the most erotic experience of his life. He felt every tiny muscle contraction as their hips moved slowly in unison, rolling and undulating in heated control. Beyond them the surf crashed into the sand and its power was incorporated into the rhythm that fed the inner music of their dance.

The camp fire, the other party goers, and the night fell away, and there was only the two of them, baring their souls as the movement of their bodies expressed their feelings with a purity that silenced the onlookers. Caitlan would have sworn that John had been drenched in liquid moonlight, and the music filled her with such wonder that she felt as if she were dancing on silk.

Then the music ended, and Caitlan and John stood silhouetted against the night sky, two lovers as one.

Caitlan looked up at John in wonder. What she felt was more than the passion of their newfound joy. From somewhere in the hidden recesses of their minds they'd reached back to a time of honesty. What she and John shared as they looked at each other went deeper than the spoken word, and nobody watching doubted the commitment they'd given by their dance.

"*Whooooee!*" A breathless voice finally broke the silence.

"I need to take a swim and cool off," another said, and the speaker came to his feet in a rush.

"Not me," a third choked out. "I have better things on my mind. Come on, woman, let's get out of here."

The party quickly broke up with half of the group heading for the water and the other half saying quick good nights to Joe.

Caitlan dropped her eyes shyly. For the first time in her life she'd allowed herself to publicly display her feelings.

John cleared his throat. He lifted Caitlan's chin and grinned foolishly. "I think we turned them on, darling. I'm sorry if I embarrassed you in front of your friends. I didn't know I could dance like that."

"Neither did I," she confessed.

John glanced around. Think about icebergs, snowstorms, your mother, he willed his reluctant body. But the touch of the woman in his arms was too powerful, and his body refused to follow directions. They were alone with only the excited shrieks of the swimmers in the water a long way down the beach.

"Let's go home," John said, lifting Caitlan into his arms.

"What are you doing?" She clung to his neck in surprise.

"Carrying you. Me Tarzan, you Jane."

"You're crazy. I feel more like Fay Wray with King Kong."

"Do you? Let me see." He picked at the knot of her sarong until it was loose. With a roar he lifted her higher so that he could complete the job with his teeth, and the sarong fluttered to the ground as he walked.

"Nope!" he exclaimed seriously. "Not Fay—Eve. This is the Garden of Eden, and you're my Eve."

"There's something wrong here," Caitlan insisted. "Put me down."

John stopped. "Why?"

"I'll show you." He complied, standing motionless as she began to lift the T-shirt from his taut body. With maddening expertise she unbuttoned, unzipped, and slid his cutoffs down his tight, muscular legs until he stood before her wearing only briefs, distorted with the evidence of his desire.

As she slid the briefs from his body he let out a deep, ragged sigh. "Yep, definitely an error here," he whispered.

"What?"

"No fig leaf, big guy," she said, then turned and ran down the beach toward the cottage.

With a mighty yell, John kicked off his shoes and ran after her, catching her before she'd taken a dozen steps. This time he put her over his shoulder, ripping the wisp of lacey panties from her body in one motion.

He turned and walked into the water with her.

"Let me up, John," she said. "The blood is rushing to my head."

He was waist-deep. "All right, Eve." He shifted her from his shoulder, allowing her to slide down his chest until her legs were around his hips and the hard, throbbing part of him was cradled by her body.

"John!" Her breath was irregular, and her body ached with the nearness of him and her newfound need. "Please!"

"You want me?" He lifted her up and down in the tantalizing promise of what was to come. "Tell me that you want me inside of you, that you want me as much as I want you. Tell me, Caitlan, my love."

Want him? She was on fire, and the water at her waist couldn't cool her. The waves crashed against them, lifting them with powerful motions. "I want you, I want you inside me. Please, John, take me into the house."

"No, not inside. Here. Now." And he lifted her up, bringing her down over him as he filled her. Like the stars above, each occupying that special space for which they'd been created, they came together, two perfectly matched beings joined into one. This was their moment—exquisite, unspoiled, full of the wonder of its newness. Without their moving, the pulsating motion of the ocean swept them together and apart until each felt release vibrate through them like the rumbling of a volcano exploding beneath the sea. And she knew that her sacrifice to the god had become a reality.

John leaned his head back and gave a cry of pure animal pleasure. He laughed and whirled Caitlan around in the water, delighting in the freedom of the night.

"No fig leaves here, Evie." He dropped his mouth to nuzzle at her breast. "Nothing but one man and one woman and the night."

"Yes, John. One man, one woman, and," she added under her breath, "one night."

Afterward they lay on the sand and identified the Big Dipper and Orion. He told her about his great fear that his father wouldn't be proud of him when he chose to attend college rather than join the military. He confessed to the pain that came when his father seemed not to care.

She tried to explain why she deliberately refused to put down real roots. How, when she and Ann left home, they'd lived in a series of run-down, cheap apartments. How Jeffrey and Ann had married, and why she'd lived with them, trying to earn her keep by going out into the community. Now she house-sat and nursed the terminally ill.

John held her close and felt the pain of her wandering. He'd never known that kind of rootlessness. From the time he was big enough to know, his life had been the Garmon Chocolate Company. Jeffrey was supposed to take the helm with John as his right arm. But the plans had changed, and John had been forced into a job he hadn't expected.

"Don't you like being in charge?" Caitlan asked, though she thought she already knew the answer.

"Yes, I guess I do. I'm good at what I do, and I feel proud about the growth of the company. We're expanding by giving our employees a part in the decision-making process. We work together, but ultimately I'm responsible. It seems to work."

"Don't you ever have doubts? I mean, in the workings of that well-oiled machine don't you ever have glitches?"

He felt her tense as she asked the seemingly unimportant question. "Yes. Of course. But very few. If you know exactly where you're going, you're more likely to get there."

"Exactly where you're going. My, my. Sounds pretty dull to me."

"Dull? No. There is a great deal of satisfaction in the completion of one's plans, in success. You know that old adage about work well done."

"I guess I measure my satisfaction on a smaller scale, John. A patient's smile, an hour without pain when they're hurting, a day of living. I'm afraid I don't know much about plans and blueprints. Life just seems to keep getting in the way."

There was a long silence. Across the heavens a plane moved slowly, its lights blinking until it was beyond the horizon.

A chill prickled Caitlan's skin.

"What's wrong, are you cold?" John pulled her closer.

"I was just thinking about a movie I saw once, where the opening credits were like the ocean. Except the water was brilliantly colored and one color spread into the other, swirling about without mixing, making designs like a kaleidoscope. That's the difference between us, John. You're a blueprint—all neatness and order—and I'm a finger painting, swirling here and there, having no plan at all."

John leaned up on his elbow and looked down at her. "Ah, but Caitlan, you give great joy and beauty to everyone who knows you."

"But what have I accomplished?"

"You've given life to a child, Caitlan Garmon, a most wonderful gift of love."

"Caitlan Garmon," she whispered. Caity's name. The name was . . . right. She wished that the look of love that had come into John's eyes was for her, then chastised herself for the selfishness of her thoughts. She'd wanted, hoped that John would care for Caity. And she'd watched that caring grow. She knew now that her wish had been granted. A deep sadness swept over her. Tomorrow, or the next day, or the next, he'd be gone. This night was all that she'd ever have.

One last time John sprang to his feet and carried her into the sea to wash the sand from their bodies. When he was satisfied that every grain had been sloughed away, he carried her into their cottage.

She buried her head in the curve of his neck and closed her eyes, trying to preserve the touch and taste of him. Through the darkness he walked, and she felt the soft ocean breeze timidly caress their bodies.

They climbed the ladder to the loft. Upstairs the king-sized mattress lay directly on the carpeted floor, covered with a soft down comforter and scattered with large pillows.

This time when they made love there was no urgency. He was gentle and slow. Each time he touched her, her joy became more intense, and the pain of her knowledge that tomorrow would come grew deeper. John finally pulled her alongside of him, resting her head on his arm and sliding her leg across him so that they were touching intimately even as they lay relaxed and still.

For the first time in his life he was about to negotiate an arrangement of the heart, and he didn't know how to approach the subject. For days he'd worked out the details. He'd planned to be businesslike, state his proposition without allowing his personal feelings to influence Caitlan. But the events of the night had ended that plan, had confused him. He was no longer sure what he felt. Caring for Caitlan had been a challenge. She'd rebuffed his help, then his advances, pushed him away, refused to acknowledge the attraction between them.

From the instant when she'd opened the door, he'd felt a great need to protect her. He'd kissed her because he wanted to make love to her. He was suspicious that what he was experiencing was more than just a reaction to being alone with Caitlan and the child. His involvement with Caitlan had stopped being a penance to his brother. Jeffrey's request was long forgotten. John wasn't playing at fatherhood. What they'd shared wasn't some erotic adventure. Was he in love at last? he wondered.

"I have to say something to you, Caitlan, and knowing the way I tend to take over and run things, I'm certain that I'll mess this up."

Caitlan steeled herself to be calm. It had come—the separation—and that was good. Being alone with John was driving her mad. She wanted him to take her into his arms and comfort her, love her. She knew he wanted her physically, and she couldn't deny her own desire any longer. But what he felt was only lust, and she wanted more. They had the night, but then it had to end.

He breathed a shaky sigh of relief. Maybe it wouldn't be as difficult as he'd envisioned. She would listen. He allowed himself to begin to hope. "I'm glad you understand. I know that tonight we've let ourselves get carried away. I mean it's only natural, living together in such a close setting. I understand that I've overwhelmed you. But . . . will you marry me, Caitlan? It's going to be hard for you to give up the life you've made here and come to Savannah. But after we're married, I promise, Mother and I won't drive you crazy."

Caitlan sat straight up. "What?"

The air whooshed out of Caitlan's lungs. Married? Why, marriage was the last thing she'd considered. Having John forever in her bed, in her life? The idea was too sinfully delicious to imagine.

"Yes, I told you I'd handle this all wrong. But would it be so bad, being Mrs. John Garmon?"

Bad? No, you fool, she wanted to shout. Marriage would be wonderful. She'd willingly die and go to heaven, if heaven meant being with him. But the cold reality of his offhand proposal sank through to her.

John sat up behind her and came to his knees, tangling his foot in the comforter, adding to the confusion.

"Surely you'd agree that marriage would be in Caity's best interest. After all, she's the only Garmon heir. One day the chocolate company will be hers. She'll have to be trained to accept that responsibility."

A Garmon, he'd said. His proposal was made in the best interest of the child. He was asking her to marry him—for the baby's sake. "Whatever gave you the idea that I would consider coming to Savannah?"

"Because it's the right thing to do. I want you there, Caitlan," he said hoarsely. "I thought, after tonight, that you might want to be with me. Am I wrong?"

Caitlan stood and walked to the window, oblivious to the tears streaming unchecked and unrecognized down her cheeks.

"You'd want me to join the Junior League, help raise money for the opera, and attend society events, wouldn't you?"

"Personally, I wouldn't care. But the Garmons have a certain responsibility to uphold tradition. I'm afraid. Caity will need to learn what will be expected of her someday. Of course, you wouldn't have to do anything you didn't want to."

"Of course not," she echoed. "Won't I muddy up your blueprint, John? I mean how do you intend to explain me—and Caity? Will she be your child, or your brother's child? Won't I be a little too much for the Garmon family to live down?"

"I don't see that there is any need to explain you at all. You'll be my wife and Caity will be our child, not Jeffrey's."

"I see. And Miss Mettie? What will you tell her?"

"The truth, Caitlan, that Caity was the result of an in vitro fertilization, that she's Ann's and Jeffrey's biological child. I know the truth, Caitlan."

"So, now that I've admitted to that little fact it's all right for us to get married—to protect Jeffrey's child?"

"I'd say that would be the proper course of action."

"Proper course? You're right there, John. I've never been able to stay on course in my life. Aside from the question of Caity, which I don't think I want to think about right now, what would Miss Mettie say if I gave away the family jewels or took in some homeless waif? Would she be proud of her daughter-in-law?"

"She probably wouldn't understand," John admitted. What was happening to his wonderful plan to make love to her and convince her that they could make a future together for themselves and the baby? He was losing her, and he didn't know how it had happened. "What my mother thinks won't matter, Caitlan. Once we are married, she'll learn what a kind, loving person you are."

"Mother Goose and Mata Hari were kind too," Caitlan said and swung around to climb down the ladder. "If and when I marry, John Garmon, it will be for love, with a man who thinks I'm the best thing since sliced bread—not out of a sense of duty to his family. Do you understand what I just said?" Caitlan yelled angrily up from the bottom of the ladder. "We're talking plain white bread, wrapped in plastic, and fastened with a twist-tie, John, not some expensive chocolate in a satin box and tied up with velvet ribbon."

Caitlan whirled around, marched into her bedroom, slammed the door and locked it behind her. No more cowboys and Indians. When the movie ended this time, the hero wouldn't stop short of riding over the cliff, the train wouldn't be prevented from smashing the wagon stalled on the railroad track. The hero wasn't going to charge to the rescue in the next episode. It was the end—of everything.

"Are you sure, Caitlan?"

John was wearing the butter-colored silk jacket, the dark navy slacks, and the Italian shoes with the tassels. He stood in the doorway, his suitcase in one hand and his briefcase in the other.

There were circles beneath his eyes, and the suggestion of stubble on his left cheek where he'd missed a streak when he'd shaved. Caitlan swallowed hard and forced air into her lungs. Before the sun rose, she'd headed down the beach away from the cottage. She'd tried to put aside her own feelings and look at the situation logically.

Granted, the Garmons did have a legal claim on Caity. The did have the wealth to give her whatever she might need. One day she might inherit a candy company. Caitlan had no doubts that John loved the child, but that was separate from their relationship. What would happen if she accepted John's offer of marriage? Could she live with a man who didn't really love her? Granted they were great in bed together, but would "great" last?

She acknowledged the truth. She wanted to be

John's wife. He didn't mean to be stuffy and dictatorial. He just didn't know any other way to be. He could change. She'd seen him do it. She'd watched her mother turn into a bitter old woman because she was forced to live alone. Would she turn against Caity as her mother had turned against her and Ann? Maybe marriage was the smart move for her to make.

But if John didn't love her and she accepted his offer, she would die. She'd never been able to lie. He'd soon know how she felt, and she couldn't face a marriage of dutiful gratitude. She'd seen the kind of love that Ann and Jeffrey shared. Marriage was what she wanted, but it had to be a real marriage. She wouldn't settle for anything else.

"I'm sure, John," she finally answered. "I won't marry you. Please go before Danni brings Caity home. I won't keep her from you or your mother. We'll work out the details as we go along. I'll agree to let you contribute to her support and have some input toward her upbringing. If and when it comes time to make a decision about the company, we'll do it. But we'll stay here, on the Carnival Strip, until Caity is old enough to decide for herself."

John hesitated. He wanted to throw Caitlan over his shoulder and lock her in his car. She belonged back in Savannah in his apartment, in his life, in his bed. Why was she refusing to see that they belonged together? He was being torn apart. "What about us?"

"Us? The us we've experienced is an illusion, John. I think that I may be falling in love with you, but I could never change into what you'd need me to be. I'm an outlaw, John. I break all the rules, and I could never do that as one of the Savannah Garmons. Thanks for the rescue attempt, cowboy. You ride your white horse very well, but there's no sunset for us to ride off into."

She started to kiss him, saw him stiffen, and stopped her movement inches away from his lips.

He froze for a moment, then dropped his cases and caught her in his arms. His kiss was harsh and urgent, and when he finally tore himself away from her, she couldn't look at the anger in his eyes. Long after she heard the sound of his motorcycle die away, she felt the imprint of his kiss. It wasn't until much later that she found the car keys and his note.

"You can keep the car or give it away. It's yours, along with my heart."

Nine

"Caitlan, you haven't been the same since you let that gorgeous man leave this cottage without taking you with him."

Danni Manderson slid her dark glasses on top of her head and drummed her long, red-tipped fingernails on the redwood table, her expression one of muted horror.

"Yes. I let him go, after . . ." Caitlan's voice was low and wooden. "No, that's not true . . . exactly. I mean I practically threw the man out. What else was I to do after I . . . well . . ." Her voice trailed off miserably.

"Am I never going to get a complete sentence out of you again?" Danni's voice was filled with exasperation. "Let me see if I can fill in the spaces. You let him make love to you, and when he didn't offer to marry you, you pitched him out."

"No, he did offer. I mean he practically insisted on

marrying me." Caitlan shifted Caity and bounced her halfheartedly on one knee.

"He made love to you and he did propose. So, what was wrong with that? Did he ravish you? Was he brutal?" Danni sighed. "I should be so lucky."

Caitlan swung Caity up and walked back inside to put her in her playpen filled with the unicorn and blue bears that John had had such pleasure in buying. He'd left his permanent imprint on the cottage, on Caity, on Danni, and on her own peace of mind.

Danni had followed her. "I'm sorry, kid. I'm an insensitive clod. Was it very bad?"

"Bad? No. It was wonderful. It was the most wonderful night of my life. But it's over. It's over, I tell you." Her voice rose, and the pain came through in her denial.

"Sure, kid," Danni put her arms around Caitlan. "Sure."

"Oh, Danni, how long does it take to get over loving somebody?"

Danni walked Caitlan back into the living room and pushed her down on the sofa. "Okay, it's confession time, kid. Tell me what happened?"

"I can't, Danni. It's too . . . personal. I keep telling myself that it was because he was the first. But that isn't true."

"*Waaait* a minute! You mean John Garmon really is Caity's father?"

"No, of course not." Caitlan gulped and reached for a tissue on the end table at her elbow.

"You just said that John was the first man you'd made love to. Oh, you mean as in *first*?"

"Yes. First and only. He is the only man I've ever wanted to make love to."

"But, Caitlan, love, you have a child who's almost five months old. Unless we're talking immaculate conception here, you're leaving out a few facts."

"Oh, I guess it doesn't make any sense. John isn't Caity's father, his brother Jeffrey was. But Jeffrey was killed in a boating accident and John thinks he has to take his brother's place."

"It gets more kinky by the minute. No wonder John checked out. No man wants to be second in line to his own brother."

"Oh, Danni, it isn't what you think. I might as well tell you the truth. Everybody in the world probably knows it by now anyway."

When she finished the story, Danni shook her head in disbelief. "Boy, the next time you decide to do a good deed for somebody, why don't you join the Girl Scouts?"

"Oh, Danni, what am I to do? I thought that once he was gone I'd get over wanting him."

"Lordy, I don't know. I've never wanted anybody that bad, I guess. Maybe he isn't having such an easy time of it either. I don't know much about John Garmon, but if what I heard about that luau was anywhere close to true, you weren't by yourself in the wanting department."

"But wanting isn't loving, is it?"

"Maybe not, kid, but in my book it's damned close. I'd suggest you keep the home fires burning. Maybe you don't know the end of this story yet. I don't believe your hero is the kind of man who gives up."

"Do you think so?" Caitlan tried to keep the eagerness from her voice. She had plunged herself into her work and into caring for Caity. But the nights were filled with memories of John. Every disc jockey on the Gulf Coast was promoting Randy Travis's new song, and Caitlan's tension built.

"John, darling, you know that I try not to interfere in your personal life. We may share the same house, but this is your apartment and I respect your privacy."

"Come in, Mother." John's hair was uncombed. His face was stubbled with beard and his feet were bare.

Mettie Garmon stood hesitantly in the doorway to John's top-floor apartment with a worried look on her face. "I never complain about your hours or your company, do I?"

"No, Mother, you never complain. So, to what do I owe the pleasure of this visit?"

"It's that song. Mind you, I like a good tune as well as anyone, but this . . . this, whatever the song is, it's driving me crazy."

"You don't recognize Randy Travis, Mother? He's the country-music artist of the year."

"No, and I don't understand your sudden attraction to cowboy movies and songs about dying of thirst either. What's wrong, John? You've been back from Florida for three weeks, and you haven't offered one word of explanation about the woman or your hibernation from the world."

"And I'm not going to, Mother. I have to work it out for myself."

"Fine. Shall I cancel the board of directors meeting that was rescheduled for this afternoon?"

John blinked his eyes and studied the date on his watch. "Rescheduled? The meeting is set for June twenty-third. Twenty-third? That was yesterday."

"Yes," Mettie agreed quietly. "And when you didn't appear, it was postponed."

"Damn! I'm sorry, Mother. I can't believe that I forgot the meeting. I don't know what's wrong with me."

"Neither do I, John, but I'm here when you decide to come back to the world and discuss the matter."

John sighed and threaded his fingers through his hair. "Thank you, Mother, for your reticence. I suppose I do owe you some kind of explanation. The woman in Jeffrey's will . . ."

"Caitlan Downey? What about her?"

"She's not what we . . . I expected. I mean she has a child."

"I assumed so, since she was very pregnant at the funeral. Why is that important to us?"

"Because . . ." John considered his answer carefully. Though he'd sworn that he was going to tell his mother about the baby, he found that he couldn't do it. He was as bound by Caitlan's promise to Jeffrey as she had been. Jeffrey had passed on his secret in the note, but it had been private, meant for his eyes only. Still, Caity was legally and morally a Garmon, and his mother had the right to know the truth.

"Because why, John?" Mettie's voice was quietly persuasive.

"Because she needs the income. Jeffrey left her the stock. He wanted her to have it," John argued, as much with himself as his mother. "I told her that we'd see that she has the income, provided she signs the control of the stock over to the family."

"Fine, if you and Jeffrey felt that was the right thing to do, I'll go along. I trust that you'll explain the situation to the board?"

"The board?" John glanced at his watch again. "Oh, yes. I'll get dressed right away. And, Mother, I'm sorry if I've worried you. I've had a lot on my mind."

"My nervous breakdown is going to be one of them if you play that song again," Mettie said under her breath.

Mettie listened to the words of the song as she stepped on the elevator and pushed the button for her apartment on the ground floor. When the music stopped abruptly, she gave a deep sigh of relief. When she heard John's steps in the marble foyer thirty minutes later, she gave a jaunty thumbs-up sign to her reflection in the antique glass mirror over the Queen Anne sideboard.

Perhaps now John would get back to his routine, and their lives would be normal again. Sooner or later she'd find out about the woman.

John returned from the meeting just in time to change and accompany her to a summer concert under the stars. The halfway point in the concert offered a selection of bittersweet love songs that didn't serve to lighten John's mood. When his mother suggested they leave after intermission, John agreed eagerly. When she explained that she'd decided to visit her sister in Miami for a few days, John agreed just as eagerly.

Mettie rang the doorbell of Caitlan's Florida beach cottage the next day. The eager yearning in the eyes of the fragile young woman who answered the door died a quick death.

"Caitlan Downey? May I come in?"

Caitlan blinked her eyes sleepily and swallowed hard. She recognized the woman standing in the sunlight and swore a silent oath.

"Uh, yes, Mrs. Garmon, come in." She stood back and watched the woman step inside, look around, and seat herself gracefully on the couch.

"I hope I'm not disturbing you, Caitlan, but I felt I had to come and see for myself why my son has become a hermit with very strange musical tastes."

Caitlan looked down at her wrinkled dress and wished she were in a gondola on some Venetian canal or in a hot-air balloon over the Mojave desert— anywhere but in the living room she'd intentionally avoided as much as possible for most of the past three weeks.

"John, a recluse?"

"Yes, he's locked himself in his apartment where he spends hours listening to the stereo. What did you do to him to change him into Howard Hughes?"

Caitlan giggled, then choked off her laughter at the bittersweet mental picture of John Garmon with great long fingernails and a flowing beard. "At least he has aristocratic knees," she said, and closed her eyes in mortified silence.

"Can't you tell me, Caitlan? I don't mean to pry, but I'm desperate. I've already lost one son. I don't want to see another one turn into a sour, lonely man."

"He'll get over it." Caitlan threaded her fingers through her hair and tried to restore some order to the dark fringe curling around her head after her walk down the beach from the highway. She'd put Caity in her playpen and had been heading into the kitchen for a bottle when the doorbell rang.

In spite of the knowledge that John wouldn't return, she couldn't keep herself from hoping. No matter what she'd hoped for, the last person in the world she expected to see was Mettie Garmon, resplendent in a pale blue shirtwaist dress and plain white low-heeled shoes. Tasteful, discreet, and concerned, the woman held her purse tightly in her hands as she tried to be polite.

The silence was broken by Caity's howl of hunger.

"Gracious, your baby sounds very angry." Mettie glanced anxiously into the adjacent room.

"Yes. She's hungry. I was just about to feed her. Do you mind?" Caitlan went into the bedroom and reappeared holding the child, who glanced at Mettie, opened her eyes in surprise, and held out her arms.

"No, Caity, Mrs. Garmon doesn't want to take you," Caitlan said and shifted the baby to her hip.

But Caity had no intention of being put off. She whirled around and let out an even louder howl of indignation.

"Sorry, Mrs. Garmon, she's used to everybody taking her automatically. She'll settle down as soon as I get her bottle." Caitlan opened the refrigerator door, took out a bottle, and started back toward a rocking chair opposite the couch.

Mrs. Garmon didn't say a word. She was staring at Caity as if she'd seen a ghost. For a long moment the child and the older woman studied each other. The next time Caity held open her arms, Mrs. Garmon dropped her purse and reached down to take her.

"May I feed her?"

Caitlan agreed and watched the older woman arrange the baby comfortably in her arms. She seemed to forget that Caitlan was there. Caitlan knew as she watched that there was some mysterious bond between the woman and the baby, something that went beyond understanding. Caity was being fed by her grandmother, laughing and cooing for the woman who dropped all her stiffness and cooed back at the child. Did she have the right to keep the two apart? Caitlan asked herself.

For the next hour, Mettie Garmon instigated a nonstop question and answer session that interspersed stories of her sons and their misadventures with a free discussion and complimentary approval of Caitlan's work as a nurse and her plans for the future of her child.

Mettie didn't ask the question that Caitlan dreaded, and Caitlan soon came to know that she didn't care who Caity's father was. It was obvious that there was an unmistakable tie that bound them, and nothing else mattered.

After the child had been put to bed for the night, the two women sat on the deck in the darkness. Comfortable with the older woman, Caitlan finally answered her original question.

"What happened was, John asked me to marry him."

"But you said no?"

"Yes, I refused."

"Why? It's obvious that he loves you."

"No, that isn't the reason he asked me. It's because of the baby. He feels responsible for Caity, that's all."

"No, I don't think so, Caitlan. I don't think that's all he's feeling. Can you tell me about it?"

"Well, maybe he does care for me—a little. But I could never be like the rest of you. Savannah is your home—not mine."

"Caitlan, you belong wherever you want to be. You're a child of life. You'd be just as loved on Wharf Street as the Carnival Strip. Don't let Jeffrey's flight from his family influence you. Jeffrey was different, and we didn't know how to love him for who he was. I hope that if I've learned anything, I've learned tolerance. My, my, don't I sound full of myself." Mettie laughed and the sound of her laughter trailed into the night.

She was right. Jeffrey and Ann were dead, but they had touched the lives of everyone they'd loved. They left Caity behind, Caity, the grandest gift of all—a gift of love to a grandmother who needed her very much. With a prayer for forgiveness to Jeffrey and Ann, Caitlan drew up her courage and told Mettie Garmon the whole truth.

She explained Ann's fear that the world would make the Garmon family front-page news if they'd discovered that Caitlan was the surrogate mother for her sister and brother-in-law. The name on the birth certificate was Caitlan Ann Garmon, the name Jeffrey and Ann had chosen. She'd planned to call the baby Ann, but it would have been too painful, so she'd chosen Caity.

Before she left the next day, Mettie hugged Caitlan and said she wouldn't interfere. John would come to his senses, sooner or later. He just had to find his own way. "But, do promise me one thing," she asked in all seriousness, "if that singer records another sad song, will you please not let John hear it?"

John Garmon paced his apartment until he couldn't stand the confinement any longer. He'd invited three different women to dinner on three different nights, kissed them each at the door and paced the floor some more. They weren't Caitlan.

Caitlan Downey wasn't some woman taking advantage of a situation. Without meaning to, she'd reached out and touched him in such an innocent, loving way that she'd changed his life. Now he was avoiding everyone. Every time he went out of his house and saw a pregnant woman or a baby, he ached inside. The woman was driving him crazy—a nurse who took in runaways, gave away ten-thousand-dollar vehicles, and arranged blind dates for the terminally ill.

He'd never planned on falling in love. He'd loved his father, who'd traveled the world as a marine and barely had been a presence in his life. He'd loved Jeffrey, who'd turned his back on the family business and with whom he hadn't reconciled before he died. Dare he love someone else?

Mettie Garmon returned home. She seemed pleasant enough to John, but she avoided his living quarters. If he heard music boxes and windup toys on his occasional late-night raids of the refrigerator, he passed it off as television commercials.

The Fourth of July came and went. Caity was probably sitting up by now, he realized, maybe even trying to stand. Was Caitlan regaining her strength? He found a television station that played Western movies, and he learned about Lash LaRue, the Cisco Kid, and Red Ryder. Caitlan was right, the hero never kissed the heroine. Damn fools, he thought. If they had a heroine like Caitlan, they wouldn't be able to stop themselves. If he had a white horse like Hop Along Cassidy, he'd ride up to her cottage, vault over that deck rail, and carry her off into the sunset.

He'd . . . Hell, what was he sitting there for when he wanted to be with Caitlan? All he needed was a certain doe-eyed woman. She was perfect just as she was. She didn't have to change. He'd be the one to change. He'd never shave again. He'd give away his Guccis, swap his Swiss watch for a Timex, and become a house husband and raise their child—all their children, he amended. Hell, Caitlan might even be pregnant. He hadn't protected her, and he didn't think she'd been prepared. What if she were pregnant? He'd better get back to Florida quickly, he decided.

But first he had to see a man about a building. There must be a warehouse somewhere on Wharf Street that had no more than four floors. If not, he'd build one.

Whistling, John met the postman coming up the walk of the Garmons' house at a dead run. He took the small package being delivered, gave the startled man a jaunty salute, and vaulted over the iron rail fence surrounding the front yard without touching the top.

The only charter service available was a helicopter company whose pilot swore that he could make the Florida Carnival Strip in two hours with the right incentive. They were on their way when John remembered the package and pulled it from his pocket.

It was addressed to Kemo Sabe Garmon in Caitlan's bold, flowing handwriting. John smiled—the Lone Ranger. He tore the paper away to reveal a small velvet box. Inside the container was a single silver bullet and a card which he read with a happy grin.

Outlaw desperately seeking masked man pledged to love, honor, and reform. She'll serve her sentence in Savannah, or anywhere else. I love you, Caitlan.

P.S. You'd better bring another car. I loaned yours to Joe.

"Yahoo!" He'd buy a dealership if that's what it took.

The startled pilot jerked the copter up and down in a motion that threatened for a moment to abort their mission.

"Hey, man, you crazy?"

"Yep, that's what I am, all right, crazy. I'm in love with a lady who gives away automobiles and has babies for love. Say, do you think you could land this tin can on a beach?"

"Man, when I was in 'Nam I landed this thing on a space you couldn't stand in. Make it worth my while, and I'll put it anywhere you say."

The drab olive helicopter wasn't a white horse, but John Garmon thought it would do just fine.

Caitlan heard the noise. She felt the noise. It vibrated the cottage and rattled the dishes in the cupboard.

"Now what?" She pulled on her old terry cloth robe and headed for the deck. Since Danni had picked up Caity thirty minutes before, it had been one thing after another. At a time when she was trying desperately to hurry, the world seemed bent on stopping her from packing. She glanced at the clothes she'd chosen and discarded, at the open suitcase on the bed, and shook her head. Her flight to Savannah left as soon as she finished her shift. She knew she was late, but surely Kelly hadn't decided to pick her up in the police helicopter.

She opened the sliding glass doors, stepped out onto the deck and was immediately caught up in the wind generated by the propellers. She held on to the rail and watched in disbelief as the machine landed and the door swung open.

"John!"

"How do you like my horse, ma'am?"

She ran down the steps and straight into his arms, still not believing that he was there.

"Gene Autry would die of envy. What took you so long?"

"I had to buy a building."

"What kind of building?"

"A warehouse with only four stories." He was content to simply hold her and breathe in the fresh, sweet smell of the woman he loved.

She looked up at him and saw the love in his eyes. "Why?"

"No more twenty-first floor, babe, you've grounded me forever."

"No! I want you to be whatever you are. Don't change for me."

"I won't," he moved an inch closer. "I'm changing—for me. You've made me feel alive. I know now what Jeff meant once when he said that life was crossing the mountain."

"So do I," she confided in a whisper. She could feel the warmth of his breath on her lips. "I bought a designer dress," she whispered. "I had my plane ticket. I was coming to you."

"Never. I want you just the way you are, barefoot." He slid his hand inside the robe and grinned. "Bare-bottomed, and wanting me."

He picked her up in his arms and kissed her all the way inside as the machine rose and rumbled across the sky. "Where's Caity?" he managed between kisses.

"With Danni. Damn!" She groaned. "I have to go to work."

"No you don't. I talked to Kelly over the helicopter's radio." He kissed her again. "He called his wife. Everyone is covering for you." He opened her robe and slid it off her shoulders as he laid her on the carpet.

"Everyone?"

"They love you." He stood and removed his shoes and shirt. His jeans and briefs followed, but he never took his eyes off the woman who was looking up at him in adoration. "And," he knelt reverently over her, "so do I, my little outlaw. The warehouse building I bought is for you. You can fill it with sick people, runaways, bag ladies, whoever you want, as long as you leave room inside for me and our children. I'm never leaving you again."

"Promise?"

"Consider yourself under my protective custody, outlaw lady—forever."

A week later they were married on the beach at sunset, surrounded by the ever-widening circle of their friends.

The mother of the groom wore a silk dress of the same color as the pink ribbon rosette pinned in the golden hair of the baby she was holding with loving care.

The bride, glowing with the magic of love, had daisies and baby's breath in her hair and wore a simple white eyelet dress. Around her neck on a silver chain hung a tiny silver bullet, which rested secretly between her breasts.

The groom looked splendid in white boots and a white linen suit. Nobody but Caitlan knew about the silver badge she'd pinned on his shirt pocket over his heart.

It didn't rain. Caitlan said it wouldn't, and nobody had doubted her for a moment.

THE EDITOR'S CORNER

Next month we celebrate our sixth year of publishing LOVESWEPT. Behind the scenes, the original team still works on the line with undiminished enthusiasm and pride. Susann is a full editor now, Nita is still the "fastest reader in the East or West," Barbara has written every single piece of back-cover copy (except the three I wrote in the first month, only proving Barbara should do them all), and from afar Elizabeth still edits one or two books each month. And I believe I can safely say that our authors' creative contributions and continuing loyalty to the line is unparalleled. From book #1 (**HEAVEN'S PRICE** by Sandra Brown) to book #329 (next month's **WAITING FOR LILA** by Billie Green) and on into the future, our authors consistently give us their best work and earn our respect and affection more each day.

Now, onward and upward for at least six more great years, here are some wonderful LOVESWEPT birthday presents for you. Joan Elliott Pickart leads off with **TO FIRST BE FRIENDS,** LOVESWEPT #324. Shep Templeton was alive! The award-winning journalist, the only man Emily Templeton had ever loved, hadn't died in the Pataguam jungle, but was coming home—only to learn his wife had divorced him. Eight months before, after a night of reckless passion, he had left for his dangerous assignment. She'd vowed then it was the last time Shep would leave her. Love for Emily was all that had kept Shep going, had made him want to live through months of pain and recovery. Now he had to fight for a new start. . . . Remember, this marvelous book is also available in a beautiful hardcover collector's edition from Doubleday.

In **BOUND TO HAPPEN,** LOVESWEPT #325, by Mary Kay McComas, a breathtaking angel drives Joe Bonner off the road, calls him a trespasser, then faints dead away in his arms. Leslie Rothe had run away from her sister's wedding in confusion, wondering if she'd ever fall

(continued)

in love—or if she even wanted to. Joe awakened turbulent emotions, teased her unmercifully, then kissed her breathless, and taught a worldly woman with an innocent heart how it felt to love a man. But could she prove how much she treasured Joe before her folly destroyed their love?

Next, we introduce an incredibly wonderful treat to you. Deborah Smith begins her Cherokee Trilogy with **SUNDANCE AND THE PRINCESS,** LOVESWEPT #325. (The second romance in the trilogy, **TEMPTING THE WOLF,** will be on sale in June; the final love story, **KAT'S TALE,** will be on sale in August.) In **SUNDANCE AND THE PRINCESS** Jeopard Surprise is Robert Redford gorgeous, a golden-haired outlaw whose enigmatic elegance enthralls Tess Gallatin, makes her want to break all the rules—and lose herself in his arms! He'd come aboard her boat pretending to court the blue-eyed Cherokee princess, but his true mission—to search for a stolen diamond—was endangered by Tess's sweet, seductive laugh. Tess could deny Jep nothing, not her deepest secrets or her mother's precious remembrance, but she never suspected her lover might betray her . . . or imagined how fierce his fury might blaze. An incandescent love story, not to be missed.

LOST IN THE WILD, LOVESWEPT #327, by Gail Douglas, features impossibly gorgeous Nick Corcoran, whose mesmerizing eyes make Tracy Carlisle shiver with desire. But her shyness around her grandfather's corporate heir apparent infuriates her! For three years Nick had considered her off limits, and besides, he had no intention of romancing the snobbish granddaughter of his powerful boss to win the top job. But when Tracy outsmarted a pair of kidnappers and led him into the forest in a desperate escape plan, Nick was enchanted by this courageous woodswoman who embraced danger and risked her life to save his. But could Tracy persuade Nick that by choice she wasn't his rival, only his prize?

(continued)

Peggy Webb gives us pure dynamite in **ANY THURS-DAY,** LOVESWEPT #328. Hannah Donovan is a sexy wildcat of a woman, Jim Roman decided as she pointed her rifle at his chest—definitely a quarry worthy of his hunt! With a devilish, devastating smile, the rugged columnist began his conquest of this beautiful Annie Oakley by kissing her with expert, knowing lips . . . and Hannah felt wicked, wanton passion brand her cool scientist's heart. Jim wore power and danger like a cloak, challenged and intrigued her as few men ever had—but she had to show him she couldn't be tamed . . . or possessed. Could they stop fighting destiny and each other long enough to bridge their separate worlds? A fabulous romance!

Remember Dr. Delilah Jones? In **WAITING FOR LILA,** LOVESWEPT #329, Billie Green returns to her characters of old for a raucous good time. Lila had special plans for the medical conference in Acapulco—this trip she was determined to bag a husband! She enlisted her best friends as matchmakers, invited them to produce the perfect candidate—rich, handsome, successful—then spotted the irresistibly virile man of her dreams all by herself. Bill Shelley was moonstruck by the elegant lady with the voice like raw silk, captivated by this mysterious, seductive angel who seemed to have been made just for him. Once he knew her secrets, could Bill convince her that nothing would keep her as safe and happy as his enduring love? A pure delight from Billie!

Enjoy!

Carolyn Nichols

Carolyn Nichols
Editor
LOVESWEPT
Bantam Books
666 Fifth Avenue
New York, NY 10103